THE CASE

OF THE *MISSING*

DEPARTMENT

HEAD

A *Walter Dure* 'HARD CASE' MYSTERY

Books by David Staats:

<u>Novels</u>:

*The Case of the Missing
Department Head*

*The Case of the Unhealthy
Health Club*

A Midsummer Night's Death

<u>Translation</u>:

The Monk's Wedding

THE CASE

OF THE MISSING

DEPARTMENT

HEAD

A *Walter Dure* 'HARD CASE' MYSTERY

Version 2.0

by David Staats

Bathysphere Books™
An imprint of Newtext Publishing™
Newark, Delaware

Published in the United States by
Bathysphere Books™
"High Pressure Fiction"ˢᴹ
An imprint of Newtext Publishing™

ISBN: 978-1-946797-05-6

Cover Design: Liam Relph

9 8 7 6 5 4 3

1.

On a Sunday evening, shortly before 7:30, Tiffany Houlihan entered the entertainment room of the large house in which she lived, scooped up the remote control from the floor, and fell into a large, upholstered chair, the one she habitually used. She flung out her right hand, pressing the red button on the remote. After a moment, the large-screen television came to life.

Advertisements were running. She settled into her chair, folding her left leg under her. An ad came on for a new miracle drug, "Astrinjalum," which would turn elderly, incontinent women into dancing queens. Even though she was younger than the targeted demographic, she watched the ad with interest. The pleated dress which the smiling, slender actress wore flared out fetchingly as she twirled around. A soothing male voice recited warnings, speaking so rapidly that the words were nearly unintelligible: "Side effects may include edema pbguttyoe insomnia irritability increased risk churgtgopel heart attacks and death."

An ad for an auto dealership came on and she pressed the mute button.

Just as the title screen for S.C.I. "Scientific Crime Investigation" came on, her husband snuck into the dim room, ducking slightly as if he were trying to avoid interfering with the light from an imaginary film projector. He sat at the very end of the sofa, several feet away from the chair in which his wife sat.

Mr. Houlihan was an odd bird. Not only was he nine years older than his wife, but he seemed to be prematurely aged. Once tall, he was now no more than middle height. Only fifty-one, he carried his large shaggy head drooping forward, and his gray hair made him look seventy. Whether standing or walking, he no longer straightened his legs fully, so that with his knees bent and his shoulders slumped, he looked something like an elongated letter "S." Although he often puttered around in the backyard, he never seemed to accomplish anything.

"Tired of making a mess outdoors?" she said without looking at him. Neither expecting nor waiting for an answer, she unmuted the television.

Soon both spouses were rapt in the mystery surrounding the death of a wealthy young woman who owned a horse farm.

After some minutes, Houlihan commented, "That's gotta be a stunt driver. Backing a pick-up with a horse trailer attached is not an easy thing."

"It's not that hard," said his wife. "With five minutes practice anyone can do it."

After two decades of marriage, Houlihan sensed the edge in the remark. First was the implication that he didn't know what he was talking about, despite the fact that for years he had been driving his pick-up truck with a shave-ice trailer hitched to it. There was also the implication that anything which he could do was something that required only insignificant skill. He could foresee that if he explained and justified what he had said, an argument would result; and he had no desire to brave his wife's flamethrower mouth. Rather than defend his statement, he emitted a small grunt and picked up the box of large wooden matches that was on the end table next to him. He dug into the front quarter pocket of his jeans and took out a small pocket knife. With this he began to shave the edges of the square matchstick to make the matchstick round and smooth. His wife turned her head towards him and said, "You just have to do that, of course." At that moment, the camera of the television show panned to the sky, and the bright blue light from the television screen lit up his wife's face in the darkened room. Houlihan shuddered and with a sudden sharp motion, pushing the knife away from him, snicked off the head of the matchstick. It flew a few feet into the room and was lost in the pile of the carpet.

The rest of the show was unenlivened by any commentary from either spouse. As soon as the perpetrator was disclosed, Howard got up and left the room, not bothering with the final wind-up of the show.

* * *

The S.C.I. show which the Houlihans had so enjoyed was being discussed the next morning in the law office of Walter Dure. Kara, the secretary/paralegal, and Ralph, the general factotum, were in the reception area chatting.

"Did you see last night's S.C.I.?" asked Kara. She was in her early 30's, and had blonde hair that hung down not quite collar length. It framed her round face, giving her something of a Dutch-boy appearance. She was all enthused about the episode of her favorite television program she had watched the night before.

"Nah, I watched the game," said Ralph, a muscular man in his late 30's who had been running to fat for some years. He had short, light dun-colored hair, and his large, blue eyes seemed perpetually startled in his red face.

"Oh, you missed it! It looked like the husband had killed the woman he had been having an affair with."

"Cleveland . . . losers! . . . they made a double play. Okay. But they had to try and make it a triple play. They made an overthrow . . . the runner advanced to second. . . . Turned out he was the winning run."

"So the prosecution got this *forensic botanist* to prove, by identifying pollen from her shoes, that the wife had been out to the farm where the murder occurred."

"Yeah." Ralph did not seem overly interested.

"But then the defense said, big deal, pollen from sycamore trees is all over the place. But the husband and the wife lived in the city, so that seemed kinda iffy."

"Yeah."

"So, get this: the prosecution gets a DNA analysis *on the pollen* and proves that it came from one specific sycamore tree that was out on the farm. It turned out it was the wife who did it."

Attorney Dure brought his long, gray face out into the reception area. He had two sheets of yellow legal paper in his hand.

"What's that about?" he asked.

"S.C.I.," said Kara. "I watched it last night."

"That's a TV show?" asked Dure.

"Right. Scientific Crime Investigation."

Dure smiled. In his shadowed face his smile gleamed like a campfire in a twilit meadow. "If it weren't for the Fifth Amendment, he said, "there would be no scientific crime investigation."

Both Kara's and Ralph's expressions registered surprised skepticism. Taking note of this, Dure said, "The Fifth Amendment is a gem and a jewel: 'No person shall be compelled in any criminal case to be a witness against himself.' In countries that don't have the Fifth Amendment – or something like it – the police and the government get lazy. Why go to all the trouble of gathering and analyzing evidence when it is so much easier to get a confession? And a confession can't be defeated. If a defendant admits he did it, that's the end of the case. It's only the Fifth Amendment, or some provision of law like it, that forces the police to investigate crime and prove a defendant guilty. So, no Fifth Amendment, no S.C.I."

Kara nodded appreciatively. "Makes sense," she said.

"Where there's no Fifth Amendment, the police become so dependent on confessions, that torture is almost inevitable. God help you if you get arrested in Cuba – or Iran or Pakistan."

Dure gave Kara the sheets of paper he had in his hand. "Type these up, would you please?"

    * * *

A few weeks later, on a balmy Thursday evening near the end of May, the Houlihans' long driveway was parked up with cars. More cars were parked at the side of the street in front of the Houlihans' house. There was one Cadillac CTS among them, but mostly there were Beemers, Audis, Lexuses, Mercedes . . . a few Acuras. Lots of vanity plates: REFORM1, IH8MYEX, STEELES . . ..

It was something of a mystery how the Houlihans could afford a house in a development as upscale as Sunderly Chase. True, Tiffany Houlihan held a responsible position as the head of the county library system and undoubtedly pulled down a respectable salary; and nobody knew how much Mr. Houlihan netted from his seasonal shave-ice business, but still . . .

Some saw an explanation of this mystery in the fact that the Houlihans had only one child, a son named

Liam, and that they had sent him to public schools and the state university; thus they had not had the large child-rearing and educational expenses that most of their neighbors shouldered. Others saw an explanation in the fact that Mrs. Houlihan was a pooh-bah in the Reform Party and that somehow her political work combined with her government employment meant that she had a large surreptitious income.

Whatever the explanation, there was no gainsaying the fact that there they were, living in a large house among the local movers and shakers in one of the exclusive and upscale developments in the town. Like most, in fact nearly all, of the residents of Sunderly Chase, the Houlihans hired a lawn-mowing service – the lots were so large that it would be unreasonable to attempt to mow them with an ordinary riding mower. The Houlihans' lot was unique in one respect: Mr. Houlihan was unwilling to eradicate the groundhogs that lived in his yard. There was even one family of the pudgy ground-dwellers living under the sun room at the back of the house, but mostly they had their dens around the borders of the yard where trees and shrubs sheltered their dens. This occasioned some resentment on the part of the neighbors, who did not like the foraging rodents coming into their yards to feed in the garden or dig holes in the lawn.

On this pleasant May evening, some thirty Reform Party activists were crammed into the Houlihans' large living room. A political assassination had just been carried out, and Tiffany Houlihan had been one of the architects of the deed. It was she, in fact, who had moved the surprise nomination from the floor which resulted in the humiliating public defeat of the slate candidate for the vice-chair position.

The dead man, one Rhys Parker, was standing at the front of the room with the in-group to which he had, until moments ago, belonged. Dressed in a well-fitting, beige-colored suit of good fabric, he had short, dark hair, was at most ten pounds overweight, and had a somewhat sweaty, oily appearance. His face was now as red as the few blotches of late acne on his cheek. He stormed across the front of the room, rudely jostling a woman in passing, and grabbed a man by his forearm. He pulled the man out of the living room into the adjacent dining room.

"I can't believe it!" he said. "*Why?* Why the hell did they do that? Everybody knew I was only standing for the position because no one else wanted it. If anyone had said anything, I would have dropped out."

"It was low," said the man.

"I am really, *really* pissed," said Rhys Parker. "Tiffany . . . Tiffany . . . I just can't believe it!"

Later that evening, after everyone had left, Mrs. Houlihan mentioned the incident to her husband. "I don't know if I like that guy any more," she said. "He looked crazy in the eyes."

Mr. Houlihan made a pretense of appearing interested and sympathetic, but he was preoccupied with getting ready for a money-making trip with his shave-ice trailer and making sure he did not forget anything.

The next day, Friday, he pulled out of the driveway with his Hawaiian shave-ice trailer. It was about a quarter past one, just after lunch. He was headed to a gun show some fifty miles away for the weekend. As he slowly accelerated, he stuck his whole arm out of the truck's window and waved to Mr. Loveless, his next-door neighbor, who was out doing yard work. Whether it was the growl of the truck's powerful engine, or the large motion of Houlihan's arm, something caused Loveless to glance towards the street. He straightened up, leaned with one arm on his rake, and raised the other arm in a return greeting. He tossed his chin up as an acknowledgment and smiled.

* * *

Dawn Parker worked in the real estate office owned by her husband, Rhys. Sometimes she manned the reception desk, but more often, she worked in her own small office, which was separated from her husband's large, corner office by a long corridor. Her desk was a disorganized mess. Towards the back of the desktop, surrounded by sloping piles of papers, was a bowl half filled with old and rotting fruit, evidence of her failed endeavor to eat a healthy diet. The fruit did not smell too pungently because it was mostly dried out. She was making phone calls, but distractedly. Between calls she thought about non-work related matters. Sighing, she twisted in both hands the pen she was using.

Exhaling heavily, she picked up the telephone receiver again and began to punch buttons on the key pad. She put the receiver to her ear, but abruptly hung it up. She rose from her desk and walked the long corridor to her husband's large office, passing a number of small offices, the doors of which stood open, showing vacant desks. "Rhys –" she said. When he looked up at her, she stopped speaking abruptly.

"Yeah, what is it?" he said, business-like, friendly.

She went further into the office and sat in the client's chair in front of his desk. She sat at a slight angle, her legs and knees pressed tightly together. She smoothed down her skirt over her thighs, watching her hands. When her hands reached her knees she looked up. "Rhys, what is the relationship between you and Tiffany Houlihan?"

A look of shock flitted across his face, like a sheet of rain chased by a gust of wind. It vanished and the corners of his mouth turned up. He shrugged his shoulders. "She played a low trick on me about the vice-chairmanship. Even though I didn't really want it, I'm sore about the way I lost it."

She looked at him steadily and intently. She was sitting stiffly upright and did not smile. "You spend a lot of time on politics," she said. "What do you do at all those meetings?"

Like all real estate agents, Rhys Parker was a quasi-public figure. His honest-looking face was displayed all around town on 'For Sale' signs and a few billboards; his smiling face showed up in the throw-away real estate magazines; and a large sign bearing the legend, 'Parker Real Estate' stretched across the facade of his real estate office. And in his case, his amateur politicking added to his public visibility. In consequence of these facts, his wife of six years was particularly sensitive to any rumors that her husband might be involved with another woman. On the other hand, political enemies have been known to start false rumors.

"Oh, you know," he said, seeming to relax, "talk, talk. Sometimes I think that's all we do."

"Is that all you do? You don't do anything else?"

A small laugh burst from him. "Yeah . . . planning, motions, rules. Yada, yada, yada."

She stared at him, not saying anything right away. The little laugh lines in her cheeks had vanished, stretched out by the pull of gravity. "You haven't answered my first question," she said in a level tone of voice that was tightly controlled.

"Huh? . . . Oh, Tiffany. She's . . . a political operative, I suppose," he said. "I have political ambitions. We work together – with others."

"That's it?"

"That's it, honey. Something's troubling you?"

"Don't you think it's time you paid more attention to your business?"

He looked at her sharply and his eyes narrowed. "What do you mean by that?" His tone was more hostile than defensive.

"The money we've been making from this brokerage has fallen each of the past three years."

"It's a cyclical business! What do you want?"

"Marilyn Zinsser told me last year was her best year ever. I don't think the market is slow."

"She's probably lying," he nearly shouted. "You know how some people exaggerate to make themselves look good."

"I think you would be happier, and so would I, if you got back to working the way you did when you first opened your office – before you got distracted by whatever the attractions are" – her tone of voice on that phrase carried an innuendo – "about politics."

His lips worked spasmodically, as he attempted an indulgent smile and a disapproving frown at the same time. After a moment he gained control of them and said, "I told you, I'm out of it. I'm not vice-president any more. I'm done." His nostrils flared.

"That's good," she said, "because I'm not going to be made a public laughingstock."

"Oh, my God, you're crazy," he said.

"If you don't fix the problem, I will," she said, with menace in her voice.

He looked down at his desk and slowly shook his head. He said nothing. The two spouses sat in silence.

Finally, Dawn got up and walked out of the office. When she reached her own, smaller office, she spent an hour and forty minutes researching on the internet.

Around noon her husband came by her office and leaned through the door, bracing himself with his arm on the door frame. "Going to lunch?" he said.

Her eyes were red and there was a little smear of dark makeup around her right eye. "Not hungry," she said. Her voice was hard and she did not look at him.

2.

Another Monday. Motes of dust drifted slowly in the sunlight that came through the front windows of the Law Office of Walter Dure. The windows were antique in appearance, but modern in construction, double-pane glazed windows that insulated the interior from both temperature and noise. A faint ticking came from the clock on the mantel above the non-working fireplace at the far end of the room. The telephone had been quiet for a couple of hours.

Kara had finished all of her urgent work, and in the mid-afternoon was updating the Criminal Law Reporter with the supplement pages that had come in the mail that day. Mr. Dure was out of the office at a court hearing. He had said he would probably be back about four. But hearings can run long.

A quiet riffling of paper softly sounded as conscientious Kara, with the fluency of long practice, rubbed up the corners of the Reporter's pages to get to the next page that needed to be replaced. A single note, soft but clear, chimed from the clock, marking the half hour. It was four-thirty, only half an hour to go.

A synthetic rattle came from the telephone. Caller ID showed "Whittaker, Cliff." One of the bigger jerks in the local bar.

"Hello," said Kara as she opened the top right drawer of her desk and took out her telephone message pad.

"Is he in?"

"Sorry, Mr. Whittaker. Can I take a message?"

"IS HE IN?"

"I'm sorry, Mr. Whittaker. He is not in. May I take a message?"

"I don't believe it. He's just avoiding me. Put him on."

"I'm sorry, Mr. Whittaker. He is out of the office. May I take a message?"

"What's his cell phone number?"

"If Mr. Dure wanted you to have his cell phone number, you would have it."

"How much does he pay you?"

"May I take a message?"

The front door to the office opened, and a man walked in.

"He knows why I'm calling," said Whittaker.

The man, dressed in faded jeans and a plaid flannel shirt, carefully closed the door behind him and approached Kara's desk – almost timidly. His large head, weighed down by a mop of gray hair, drooped forward.

"My job is to take a message – if I can. If it's something important, Mr. Whittaker, Mr. Dure might give the call priority – of course, I can't promise; he does have a number of messages on his desk already."

"I'll bet. Maybe I'll have to come over there." Click!

Kara hung up the receiver, took a deep breath and exhaled heavily. The man who had entered was standing halfway between her desk and the door. His stance was an odd slouch. "Yes, sir. May I help you?" said Kara.

The man's head bobbed up, as if he were startled, and he approached Kara's desk. He wore a heavy leather belt, smooth and shiny, like seasoned saddle leather; a roll of belly fat bulged out above it. On the right leg of his jeans, over the thigh, was a large brownish stain that in outline resembled a skull.

"Hi. Is Mr. Dure in?" said the man in a loud voice. His wide open brown eyes blinked and his face flinched. In a more subdued tone he added, "I really hope I can see him this afternoon."

"I'm sorry he's not in at the moment. Did you have an appointment?"

"Oh, no! No, I haven't spoken with him. No, I just really need to talk to a good attorney . . .."

"I didn't know if maybe you had spoken with him directly and had gotten an appointment that I didn't know about."

"No, no."

"He's not in right now, but I expect him soon. Your name is . . . ?"

"Houlihan. Howard Houlihan."

"When he comes back, I know he has a number of things waiting for him. I don't know that he would be able to see you. He usually sees clients by appointment. Can I look at his calendar for you, in case he can't see you when he comes in?"

"No . . . no, I don't know what I'd do . . . if it's alright, I'll just wait over here?" he indicated by pointing his head and his shoulder, already taking a half step towards the waiting area.

"Sure. Okay . . .." Kara wanted to say something more, but the man was scooting over to the waiting area, keeping his head down and his legs bent, as if he were ducking under a low door frame, or trying somehow to make his way without being observed. It did not seem as if anything she might say would make a difference.

He sat in one of the two club chairs, ignoring the two upholstered arm chairs and the English roll arm sofa which stood against one wall. Kara resumed her work replacing pages in the Criminal Law Reporter. The quietude set in again. The dust motes swirled for a few minutes, then settled back into their routine of gradual drift.

"I heard he's the best lawyer in town," called out Mr. Houlihan, suddenly.

Kara shot a questioning look at the man. He certainly seemed an odd one. But, you see all kinds. "If I were in trouble," she said, "there's no one I would rather represent me. Of course, if you want a municipal bond financing, there are other lawyers." Her idea of humor.

"Right," said the man.

Kara snapped the loose-leaf mechanism of the Reporter shut and clicked the lock. She took the pile of superseded pages she had removed and slid it into the waste basket. A shadow crossed the front window and Howard Houlihan looked up.

In through the front door came a large man, heavy of build, but muscular, not fat. On second glance, one would say muscular but with an overlay of fat, like a football player a couple of years after retiring from the game. He came in with a familiar, confident air, as if he were entering his own house.

"Hi, Kara," said the husky man in a husky voice. "Got everything done." He did not notice the potential client sitting in the waiting area.

Kara nodded and smiled. "Hey, Ralph," she said.

Ralph had a large head which seemed to be red all over. The most striking thing about that florid face was the large, vivid blue eyes, which, with white showing all around the iris, gave the man an appearance, somehow, of innocence. He breezed past Kara, opened a door that led to the offices in the rear of the suite, and was gone.

"You sure you don't want me to make an appointment for you? said Kara to Mr. Houlihan, sensing that the man was becoming anxious, even though he had been waiting no more than ten minutes. "That way you wouldn't have to wait."

"He'll be in soon, you think?" said Mr. Houlihan.

"Any time now I expect him."

"I'll wait," he said, with an ingratiating smile. "It's not a problem." He dipped his head forward in a strange gesture.

Ralph came back out into the reception area. He swiveled his head, looking around as if he had lost something. He noticed Mr. Houlihan. "Hi, I'm Ralph," he said, approaching Mr. Houlihan. "You waitin' to see Mr. Dure?"

Kara cringed. She was by now familiar with Ralph's restless, almost nosy, curiosity. She thought Ralph's unsophisticated 'Hey buddy' attitude was damaging to Mr. Dure's professional image. Not to mention that Ralph seemed to have no concept of client confidentiality and the idea that if you didn't need to know something about a client, then it was best not to know it. Dure had hired Ralph seven months ago, not quite as an act of charity. Ralph had been a bricklayer who had been broadsided in a car accident. Dure had represented him and gotten a good settlement for him. But Ralph's back and shoulder had been severely injured in the accident, and he could no longer work as a bricklayer. So Dure hired him as a general factotum. He had a kind of down-to-earth practical mind. Ralph was always chatting up people, including clients, and asking the most awkward questions. She hoped he would not drive this client away.

Ralph sat down heavily on the sofa next to Mr. Houlihan. "Got a legal problem, huh?" he said.

"Yes, well, that's something I'm waiting to see," said Houlihan.

"He's smart," said Ralph, gesturing with his head towards the back, in the direction of Dure's office and tapping his temple with his finger. The expression on his face denoted that he was a connoisseur of genius on whose opinion one could rely implicitly.

"Ralph," called Kara, "would you mind taking these treatises back to the library?" She was trying to get him out of the waiting area and away from the potential client.

"Yeah, Kara. Got it, no problem," said Ralph. But he did not get up. "Ever been in trouble before?" he asked Houlihan.

Kara stood at her desk. She held her pen between two fingers in such a way that she could make it rapidly oscillate, and she made the top end of the pen whack against the cover of the treatise in the little stack on her desk, taptaptaptaptap.

"No, not really," said Houlihan, now seeming to want to shut down the conversation.

Again a shadow passed in front of the window. A tall man wearing a glum expression entered. His head was bent forward in a habitual way of walking as if he were intent on the ground before him. Dure had been remarkably handsome as a young man, tall and ruddy, with thick, dark, wavy hair; but the stress of his hard-driving legal practice had aged him. Now his complexion had a gray tinge, and the large, deep-descending circles under his eyes had become a permanent feature of his face. These dark circles, however, made his luminous hazel eyes appear even more striking.

He took two strides into the reception area and, as if startled by something, stopped dead. His long, slender, wing-tip clad foot landed flat on the floor with a thump. He looked up, turning his head to gaze into the waiting area. Seeing his man Ralph and a stranger, he smiled a smile of improbably straight, even, white teeth.

He had gotten those teeth in the Marine Corps. He had grown up poor and scrawny in that part of mountainous Kentucky where there was no coal mining, just debt-accumulating agriculture and food stamps and welfare. Shortly after he graduated from high school, Dure got on a bus which took him to a Marine Corps induction center.

During the first week of boot camp, the camp dentist extracted all of Dure's cavity-riddled teeth during a single marathon session. Later that same day, he had to stand in formation for forty-five minutes, and as the anesthetic wore off, the pain grew and he began to feel woozy. His mouth was filled with blood, but he could not spit in formation; he swayed on his feet, but he did not fall and he did not spit. The other recruits made brutal fun of his toothless gums until the full-plate dentures came in. During the thirteen-week boot camp, Dure put on 27 pounds of hard muscle, but his mental and psychological hardening occurred to a much greater degree than his physical hardening. Perhaps as a memento, after his four-year enlistment was up, he kept that set of white, even, perfectly aligned, false teeth which had been fabricated to military specifications.

Without putting down his briefcase, he went over to Houlihan, introduced himself, and told him that he could see him in a few minutes.

Kara showed Mr. Houlihan into Dure's office. Houlihan crossed the threshold, dipping his head as he did so, and stepped quickly and gingerly into the office, as if he wanted somehow to move from the door to the client chair unobserved. Once seated he let out a great sigh.

"What can I do for you?" said Dure.

"I think I need help," said Mr. Houlihan. His hands were uneasily resting on his knees. He looked like he wished he had a hat with which he could fidget.

Dure nodded. "Tell me what's bothering you."

Mr. Houlihan trembled slightly as he began speaking. "The police have been at my house all afternoon." He paused, perhaps to gauge how much sympathy he was getting. Dure's expression was attentive but impassive. "I came home this morning, just before lunch. When I drove into the driveway, I saw some buzzards in the back yard. I wondered what they could be doing – you don't see, at least I haven't seen, buzzards in my back yard." He cleared his throat. "I went back there and the buzzards flew off but they didn't go far and sat in nearby trees and it was a body. I didn't look any closer, but went into the house and called the police."

Dure interrupted. "It was a dead human being?"

"Yes, sir."

"And the police have questioned you in connection with that?"

"Yes, sir."

"Do you want me to represent you?"

"Yes, sir. That is why I am here. I need somebody to represent me. I don't want to be put in prison."

"Excuse me, then, for a moment, while I place a call," said Dure.

Dure took up the telephone handset and punched a pre-set button. "Mr. Preston, please," he said. After a moment: "Roderick, you handling the Houlihan case?"

The voice coming out of the phone was loud enough to be heard in the room. "I am aware of a homicide with that name, but the police have made no arrest, and so there is no case as far as I am concerned."

"Mr. Houlihan has retained me. We want our medical examiner to be present when you have your guy do the examination."

"As you know, Walter, that is being handled by the police homicide investigation unit. If the exam's already been started, nothing we can do."

"If it's already been started, you stop it until our guy gets there."

"I'll do what I can for you, Walter. But I can't make promises."

"You'll look bad if at some later time I bring this conversation to the court's attention."

"So your guy did it, huh?"

"I doubt it, but the facts are yet to be determined. I'm protecting his interests. It's going to be Doctor Mulvaney. I'll call him now, but you make sure your guy waits for him."

Dure called Dr. Mulvaney. Then he called in Kara and dictated a short letter memorializing his conversation with the county prosecutor, and told her to fax it to Mr. Preston.

"Mr. Houlihan, I ask your pardon for that interruption, but I wanted to get that matter taken care of before the 5:00 closing hour. In some matters, one has to move quickly. Now, you were saying that you had called the police . . .."

"They sent out two cars. And in the meantime, I called my wife, but she wasn't at work." At this point, he stopped and looked like he was going to break down.

"It was my wife. And I didn't know what to do. An ambulance came. They took her and the police asked me a lot of questions. I don't want to go to jail." Here Mr. Houlihan stopped.

"I will help you," said Dure.

"I've heard that you're good," said Houlihan.

Dure bowed his head slightly and bit his lip in acknowledgment of the compliment. "Tell me exactly what you saw," said Dure.

"After I called the police, and after I found out that my wife was not at work, I became afraid – afraid it was her. I went back out into the yard to try to look at the body. But it was too terrible. I didn't get any closer than thirty feet. The buzzards had torn the clothing and attacked the body. From my angle, I couldn't see the head, but the clothes looked like they could have been my wife's, so I couldn't look anymore. I went back into the house and called my wife's work again."

"Go on."

"They said – when I first called, the operator just said she wasn't in – but now I talked to her secretary and asked had my wife been in that day, and said no.

"Where does your wife work?"

"She's the head of the county library system."

"Then what did you do?"

"By then the police were just arriving. I had been thinking that since she scheduled the Friday before off, and since I was away the whole weekend, she might have gone for a short vacation herself. But I hadn't heard from her.

"I wanted to watch what the police did – from a distance, but they wouldn't let me. They kept me in the house asking questions."

Dure asked what the police had asked and what Houlihan had said in response. Houlihan told him the following: His wife's name was Tiffany Houlihan; they had been married for going on 24 years; they had one son, named Liam; Liam was 23 years old, had graduated from the local college, and was now working part-time at a deli called Sam's Whiches; Liam did not live with his parents, but shared an apartment with a friend; Mr. Houlihan had left home with his Shave-Ice trailer about 1:15 Friday, right after lunch; he had driven about fifty miles south and had set up in the parking lot at a week-end gun show; he had stayed at the gun show all weekend and had driven back that morning, arriving home about 11:00 a.m., as he had earlier said, and from there things were as he had said earlier, seeing the buzzards, calling the police, etc. He had a happy marriage, got along with his wife; could not think of anyone who would want to hurt him or his wife; did not know of any reason why anyone would want to kill her; probably in light of the mutilated state of the body, she would be cremated, which is what he thinks she would have wanted anyway.

Dure seemed to be finished with his questions. He paused and seemed to be thinking. "One last thing," he said, "did you kill your wife?"

Houlihan's head flew up and back as if someone had struck him. He opened his eyes wide. "No, no. No," he said, shaking his head.

"Alright," said Dure.

He had the client sign a representation agreement and set the retainer at five thousand dollars. "If I have to go into court, my fee will be one hundred thousand dollars, but until that time five thousand will suffice."

"Do you want me to pay you now?" asked Houlihan?

"Pay my secretary. We will talk more later." He paused before standing up. "Important: Don't talk to anyone about the case. No one. Not the police. Not your family. No one other than me. Do you understand?"

"Yes, sir," said Houlihan, "but I've already talked to the police."

"We will deal with that. No more. No talking. You've got it?"

"Understood, sir."

Some patients don't comply with prescribed treatment, causing headaches for doctors.

Some clients don't follow legal advice, causing headaches for lawyers.

3.

After the interview, Houlihan drove to his house in a late-model, nice-looking Ford F-250 with a double cab. Dure and Ralph followed in Dure's car to inspect the scene of the crime.

Ralph was comfortable and confident behind the wheel. As he drove, Dure told him the main points of the interview and asked him what he thought of the case. Ralph said, "You've got a guy, comes in says he doesn't want to go to jail, pays you five thousand dollars even though he hasn't been arrested?"

"Mr. Houlihan seems a fearful man," said Dure.

"Yeah 'cause he's carrying a load," said Ralph. "You don't put money out like than unless you've got a diaper full."

"He said he was away all weekend with his vending trailer," continued Dure, sitting half sideways in the passenger seat, as if he were on the sofa in his living room, having an intimate chat. "If we can prove that, it may be a good alibi. Since the police have not arrested our client, they don't think they have enough evidence to make a case. At this stage, I want to do two things: nail down our client's alibi, and find out what we can about the deceased. This case may never come to trial, but we should do certain minimally essential preparation – just in case." After a moment, he straightened in his seat and gave his attention to the passing scenery.

With the waning rush-hour traffic, it took them about twenty minutes to reach Sunderly Chase. Dead center at the front of the median strip dividing the entrance road to the development was a sign on which was written in forbidding capital letters:

A DEED-RESTRICTED COMMUNITY
NO SOLICITING
24-HOUR SURVEILLANCE

They drove past large houses on large lots. They must have been at least an acre.

Sunderly Chase was like an ice maiden, beautiful, but cold. The large, dark-windowed houses, each one a unique design, with a sort of English Gothic motif predominant, were set well back from the road, and the large lots seemed all to have been professionally landscaped. Every neatly mown lawn showed the crosshatch pattern of the large power mowers used by landscaping companies.

They followed Houlihan down a long, curving road for perhaps half a mile, then turned right onto another gently curving road, which after a quarter of a mile, with a mere two houses on each side, branched in two. They took the left-hand branch onto yet another curving road which turned out to be a cul-de-sac. It had five houses on the outside-of-the-curve side of the street, and three houses on the inside-of-the-curve side. They stopped at the third house on the outside side. Yellow plastic police-line tape was up all around the house.

The neighborhood was as quiet and apparently deserted as a ghost town. In the driveway of the Houlihans' house sat a trailer painted in many tropical colors and bearing the slogan, "Hawaiian Shave-Ice." The house was not the largest in the neighborhood, but it was large enough. It appeared to be as well kept up as the others. The yard was neat, and the plantings seemed to have been professionally chosen and maintained.

They climbed out of their vehicles into the quiet and congregated. "You don't leave that trailer out in this neighborhood?" said Dure.

"No," said Houlihan. "I keep it in the garage."

"Where the body?" said Dure.

Houlihan walked toward the driveway to his house. When he got to the foot of the driveway, where police tape blocked further access, he pointed towards the rear of the lot, along a row of plantings between his house and the next. "Back there. You can see the extra loop of police tape around where . . . the body was found."

"Ralph, take photographs," said Dure.

Dure went up to the police-line tape and peered at the place indicated. There was not much to see from that distance. It was probably forty yards from the edge of the street to where the smaller circle of tape was.

He got on his phone, called the prosecutor again. "Roderick? . . . When are they going to take the police tape down?"

"I have no control over that."

"Okay if we go in?"

"If you go in and tamper with the scene, you'll look bad if at some later time I bring that fact to the court's attention."

"Of course we won't tamper with the scene."

"If you go in, you're tampering with the scene."

"Did you get the medical examiner situation arranged?"

"We're working on it."

"Thank you, Mr. Preston."

Dure clicked off the call. "How about your neighbor?" he said to Houlihan. "Will he let us go on his property where we can get a closer view of the place where the body was?"

"He's a good neighbor," said Houlihan. "Probably."

There were enough tall trees in that part of the neighborhood that shadows cast by the slanting evening sun put the house next door entirely in shade.

"This is the Loveless's house," said Houlihan, as they were walking along the street to the next driveway. "He's a widower, now." After a pause he added, "So am I . . . now," and he looked very sad.

Brush strokes from the most recent application of rubberized driveway sealant were visible in the Loveless's neat, black driveway as they footed slowly to the walkway that led to the front door.

Houlihan rang the bell, and in a moment came the sound of a thump and of air being drawn in around the edges of the all-glass storm door. The heavy wooden door swung open to reveal an elderly man of upright bearing. The storm door was sparkling clean and transparent. A small, sad smile briefly graced the man's face as he recognized Houlihan, and he eagerly reached forward to unlatch the storm door while at the same time taking in Dure and Ralph. "Howard," he said, "I'm so sorry to hear about what happened. How are you? Come in."

He was a tall man, about seventy, with a weathered face.

"No, no. Thank you, Everett, but if you don't mind . . . what we'd like to do is walk in your yard . . . this gentleman wants to get a closer look at the place where . . . .." Apparently walking and talking were reviving Houlihan's spirits, or distracting him, or something. He stood with his hands in the quarter pockets of his jeans as if he were discussing the weather.

The man hesitated, glancing at Dure. Taking the cue, Houlihan introduced Dure.

"Alright, I'll show you," said Loveless. He came out onto the small porch and the four of them walked around to the side yard.

Mr. Loveless and Houlihan led the way to a spot between the two houses where there were some evergreen trees and a large rhododendron. Stretched out parallel to the property line was the silhouette of a body. It looked like it had been done with some kind of white spray paint. Where the head would have been was a hole in the ground and raw earth, not of recent digging, in a small pile in front of the hole. The little mound of earth at the mouth of the hole was darkly discolored. This hole was slightly under the rhododendron, and from the hole, the silhouette stretched toward the street. Half of the white marking was in the grass towards the Houlihans' house, and half was in the mulch bed that ran between the rhododendron and the nearest evergreen tree. This margin between grass and mulch bisected the silhouette lengthwise.

Mr. Houlihan was breathing heavily, as if under strong emotion.

Dure went up to the yellow tape that stretched between the trees and gazed at the site. It was about six feet inside the border formed by the tape. He pointed with his toe to a carmine-colored mushroom. "Some kind of *Russula*," he said. The other three men had blank looks on their faces, and said nothing.

"This is where the body was found?" asked Dure.

Houlihan nodded.

"Where's the property line?" he asked, looking at Mr. Loveless.

Mr. Loveless looked at Houlihan and the latter answered. "It's somewhere between this tape and the groundhog hole there. Wouldn't you say, Everett?"

It seemed for a moment that Loveless hadn't heard the question. Then he said, "I think that's about right."

"Did you see or hear anything?" said Dure to Loveless.

"No, I didn't hear anything. I was shocked when the police came." Loveless shook his head and frowned.

Ralph had been taking pictures.

They all stayed there another few minutes, staring. Dure looked around, seeming to measure an imaginary line between the Loveless house and the Houlihan house. The Loveless house was larger and extended further towards the back of the lot. A line of trees and shrubs ran along the border between the two lots. Dure stepped towards the back of the lot and sighted a line from the place where the body had been located to the back corner of the Houlihan house.

"Thank you for letting us enter upon your property," said Dure.

The laconic Mr. Loveless nodded.

"Would you mind if we came and spoke to you again about this matter?"

"That would be alright."

They were walking back the way they came. The air of the early June evening was getting cooler. At the porch, Loveless said to Houlihan, "Sorry about your wife, Howard."

"Thank you Everett," said Houlihan, in a loud voice that seemed just barely under control. He spread his hands as if to say, what can you do?

"Your house is off limits," said Dure to Houlihan as they walked. Where will you sleep tonight?"

"I'll sleep in the cab of my truck," was the answer. "It's what I do when I go out on the road. It's all set up for it."

"Oh, yes. You take that trailer out to shows. I remember that you told us that."

* * *

Ralph, driving out of Sunderly Chase with Dure riding shotgun, stopped at the intersection with the main road. On each corner stood a substantial masonry wall of colorful field stone into which was set a large stone slab, carved in the manner of a tombstone with the name SUNDERLY CHASE. He turned onto the country road and they were driving down a long hill.

Dure's cell phone rang.

"Mr. Dure, Doctor Mulvaney," said the voice on the phone.

Dure anticipated the doctor's first words. "A well-nourished white female," he said. "Go ahead."

The doctor recited his report: "Probable cause of death: decapitation. The body was not in good condition. There was animal or vulture molestation of the corpse in addition to the decapitation. Because of the exsanguination secondary to the decapitation, interpreting the pattern of lividity is problematic and thus determining a time of death is problematic. Also, the exsanguination was incomplete, but whether that is because the neck of the corpse was resting on the little mound at the opening of the animal den, or whether the corpse might have rested in some other place until the body had cooled and coagulation occurred is uncertain. The Commonwealth Medical Examiner opines, and I am inclined to agree, that time of death was either Friday or Saturday. Perhaps checking the weather records for Friday through Monday, especially the temperatures, might help us narrow it down, but I doubt it. Fortunately, the body was in a face-down position, so that the animals – or vultures – did not disturb the stomach or its contents. It appears that the deceased died within 90 to 150 minutes after a meal, probably lunch, although further analysis of the contents of the stomach together with information about the dietary habits of the deceased will strengthen or weaken this conclusion. Tentative conclusion for now: time of death probably between noon and three o'clock either Friday or Saturday, assuming the meal was lunch; however, the meal might possibly have been breakfast, so the outside limits of the time of death are 9:00 a.m. on Friday to 5:00 p.m. on Saturday. My personal opinion is that between noon and 3:00 on Friday is the most probable time."

"Thank you, doctor. Send me your written report."

"One other thing. There did not appear to be any signs of struggle. We are going to analyze the scrapings from under the fingernails, but to me the visual inspection did not make it look like anything is going to turn up from that."

"Thank you, doctor." Dure clicked off the call. "That was not helpful for our client," he said to Ralph. "He told us he left home about 1:15 on Friday. That leaves him at home during the period of time most likely to have been the time of death." He seemed thoughtful for a moment. "They haven't arrested him, and it is always to be kept in mind that we – that if the police should arrest him – we don't have to prove that someone else did it, we only have to keep the prosecution from proving that our client did."

* * *

The next morning, Houlihan brought in the five thousand dollar retainer, all in cash, in twenty dollar bills. Kara counted it and made up a deposit slip. Dure sent her immediately to the bank; he did not want a large amount of cash in the office.

After lunch, Dure had to go to court, just across the street, while Ralph made photocopies of exhibits for another case. About two o'clock Dure came back. He talked with his secretary for a few minutes in his office, then came out and told Ralph that they were going to visit the County Services Building.

That grand edifice was out of town in an inconvenient location, all by itself. It was very nearly cubic in shape, six stories high, with windows and synthetic stone on the exterior, and surrounded by an enormous parking lot.

On account of the misdirection and rigmarole that they encountered, it was some twenty-five minutes before they came to be seated in the office next to the office of the deceased Mrs. Houlihan. Located along the back wall of the fifth floor of the County Services Building were two offices with large windows facing a large, carpeted, open area. One of them was Mrs. Houlihan's office, and the other belonged to a slender woman, perhaps about forty, with large, dark eyes and sunken cheeks. She wore no wedding band, but she had a silver ring on her right thumb. The name plate next to the door read "Nan Shuettler."

Dure introduced himself. She invited him and Ralph to sit. "We are still in shock," she said. "I mean, she was just here on Thursday, and now it's what, Wednes-- no, Tuesday. So the police said she probably was –" here she made her voice a whisper "you know . . . killed –" her voice came back up, "on – well, they weren't real clear on it, but Friday or Saturday I think it was. And they were here for like two hours this morning, asking everybody questions. My cousin is a police officer, works in a small town in Tennessee. I don't think he's ever done a murder investigation. Of course, he's younger, and they don't have so many murders down where he lives. Only fourteen hundred people in his town. But there's drugs there, so you never can tell. Used to be moonshine was the thing down there, but he tells me now it's all kinds of drugs, Oxycontin and heroin and things I don't even know what they are. Isn't that a big problem that we have, with all the drugs? I mean, last week two people – two! – were murdered over in –"

Dure interrupted. "Ms. Shuettler," he said, "Since you mention it, do you think Mrs. Houlihan was involved with drugs?"

"Oh my goodness, no! I mean, I wouldn't know. I mean, I only see her around here, I don't know what she does when she's not at work. She was always nice to me. I never saw her what you would call drugged up. I mean, sometimes she would be kind of snippy, but that's not a drug effect, is it? The only thing I could say, is that, you know, sometimes, like we would be having a normal conversation, and she would just get up and leave. Right in the middle of it! So that was strange, but that doesn't mean that somebody is on drugs, I don't think. Not that I know, really, what people on drugs are like, I mean --"

Dure interrupted again. "Did Mrs. Houlihan have enemies that you know of?"

"Oh, the police asked that very same question. Enemies! That's such a, a . . . *melodramatic* word." She giggled. "No, I told them I didn't know of any *enemies*."

Ms. Shuettler drew a breath, and Dure, fearful that she would start off on another ramble, quickly put in his next question, "Had she had any run-ins, arguments, say, bitter disputes with anyone in the recent past?"

"Oh, yes!" she said, as if she were a race horse and Dure had just sounded the starting bell. "Oh-h-h, yes, there was one. It was about eleven o'clock last Thursday when she had a visitor – a stranger, apparently a member of the public. It is quite unusual for a member of the public to come to visit the County Library Department. The man stuck his arm in her office to rap on the open door, then just walked in. It was just right next door, and I could hear everything, especially since they were talking mostly in loud voices. The man was heavy set, stood about middle height, and he had thick, dark, wavy hair. 'I've got a bone to pick with you,' I heard him say.

"Tiffany said something, and the man said something that sounded like, Snodhuis, or Snodhoose, and then he said, 'Bruno.' It was the man's name, don't you think?"

"A reasonable assumption," agreed Dure.

"So I heard them talking about library rules and I heard the Greenback Party mentioned. Something about their members meeting at the Walnut Street branch, and having gotten kicked out.

"So they were arguing about the rules and the man's voice was becoming loud. 'Not what your rules say,' I heard him say. Tiffany's voice was getting loud, too. She said she wouldn't interfere with the librarian at the site.

Then the man said, getting even louder. 'I've looked you up. You and the whole lot of you are Reform Party, as is the county commissioner. The whole county government is corrupt. You just want to harass Greenback Party members.'

"Tiffany shouted, 'The rules apply to everybody.'

"And then the man said, "YOU'RE A LIAR! You and your corrupt one-party rule . . .."

"And they began yelling at the same time and I couldn't understand what they were saying. Suddenly it was quiet, and the man was outside her office. 'You'll find out,' the man said. This he didn't yell. It was more like a growl. As he passed my door, I saw his face was red."

"You said the man's name earlier. Do you know how to spell it?" asked Dure.

Ms. Shuettler shook her head emphatically, swiveling it from side to side.

Dure asked: "Who is the person who is going to take over Mrs. Houlihan's job?"

"It could be . . . maybe, you know, there are eight branch libraries and it could be the head librarian from one of those . . . or it could be – well, maybe the head librarian at the main branch. And there's Meghan Rittersreiter, the head of the Acquisitions Department. And you know, it's a good question – I'd like to know myself." Laughing a sort of a giggle, as if she were doing something naughty, she picked up her telephone and punched in four numbers. "Hi, Jennifer. . . . Yeah, yeah, I *know.* Isn't that crazy? . . . He did? When did he do that? . . . *Really?* . . . Well, you know how men are. . . ."

Two minutes later, Ms. Shuettler was still talking, apparently having forgotten about her visitors. Dure began to get out of his chair. Perceiving what he was about, Ralph stood. Ms. Shuettler motioned to them to stay, and seeing that Dure was continuing his process of standing up, put her hand over the receiver and whispered, "I'll be just another minute. Jennifer likes to talk."

Having gained his feet, Dure silently left the office.

* * *

The next morning Dure had other matters to attend to, and it was not until the afternoon that he could devote some time to the Houlihan case. Ralph drove him out to Sunderly Chase again to speak with such of the neighbors as might be home.

The police-line tape was gone and so was the shave-ice trailer. Ralph pulled into the driveway of the Houlihans' house. He accompanied Dure in walking back to the place where the body was found. Other than by the white outline on the ground, one would never know that a dead body had lain there. There was no flattening of the grass, no disturbance in the chipped bark mulch, nothing that would indicate that some 72 hours ago, a corpse had lain there, food for wild beasts.

They looked down the groundhog hole. No head was in there, but an irregular dark stain sullied the sloping side of the tunnel.

They traipsed over to Mr. Loveless's house. He was at home and invited them in. The house was neat and quiet, the way a lot of old people's houses are. The living room was a large expanse of light gray wall-to-wall carpeting. Against the back wall was a sofa; and, on either side of the picture window in the front wall, a pair of upholstered chairs. The far wall was completely book shelves, with not many books; a few knickknacks and colored vases punctuated the mostly empty, white shelves. A coffee table was in front of the sofa; on it sat a folio-sized Audubon. A small desk and straight back chair occupied a corner.

Mr. Loveless sat on the sofa. Dure and Ralph sat in the two upholstered chairs. Loveless had a large, open face. "Yesterday when you were here," he said, "I didn't want to say much because Mr. Houlihan was with you. You understand."

"Of course," said Dure.

In response to Dure's questions, he said that he and the Houlihans had been neighbors for fourteen years. He did not know of any enemies the family had. It was a good neighborhood, although not an intimate one. People kept pretty much to themselves, he said.

Mr. Loveless, leaning forward as he sat, said in a voice much quieter than he had been using, "I have long thought that something was not quite right over there." He paused. "I think father and son are both scared to death of that woman. Once I heard her screaming at him in the backyard. It was the most violent yelling I've ever heard. And another couple of times I heard similar screaming from her – when she was inside the house, no less. I was outside in my yard, and I could hear her from inside their house. Now, this is only three times over the course of some fourteen years, but the violence of her screaming was beyond anything I have ever heard."

"Do you recall what the screaming was about?" said Dure.

"I could not make out more than a word or two from the backyard argument, and nothing from the indoors ones. So, no, I don't know. But what makes me think it is something more than just ordinary argument is that both Howard and his son suffer from migraines. And they seem just beaten down. You must have noticed it yourself. I think they both have been so bullied by her that they have gotten physically ill."

Dure nodded.

"That, by the way, is why – just my opinion – Howard runs that shave-ice cart that he does. Because of his migraine attacks, he can't hold a regular job, and then taking the cart out to shows and festivals and such, lets him get away from her. And their son, Liam, he can't hold a regular job either and I suspect it's for the same reason." Mr. Loveless sat back in his chair, as if to say, Now I have told you everything; do with it what you will.

"Thank you for your candor," said Dure "I don't see any need to disclose any of this to Mr. Houlihan. It may become necessary later, however. Or it may not."

Mr. Loveless turned his hands up and made a grimace, as if to say, What can you do? I've done my duty.

"Since you have been so forthcoming," said Dure, "you won't mind a few last questions? Routine." Dure briefly put the standard questions: Did you see anything out of the usual? Did you hear anything? Did you notice any strangers in the neighborhood? All of which got negative responses.

Dure turned to Ralph. "You can put your notebook away," he said. "I think we're finished here. We don't need to trouble Mr. Loveless any further."

* * *

As Dure and Ralph were getting back into his car, a large black SUV was coming down the street. They paused to watch it. It slowed and then pulled into the driveway of the house across the street.

Dure had elicited information from Mr. Houlihan about the other neighbors. Across the street, where the SUV had pulled in, lived the Sweets – husband, wife, and two daughters. Out of the black SUV climbed a woman, and from the back seat came two teenage girls.

Dure walked briskly across the street. Ralph had to hustle to keep up. Dure rang the bell, and in a moment the door opened, but not very wide.

"I'm sure you can understand," said the woman, "after what's happened, the whole neighborhood is on edge."

She said they could come back and talk to her husband when he got home.

They drove the short distance to the Vanderlogens, but there was no car in the driveway, the curtains were drawn, and there was no answer at the door.

* * *

After the interview with Mr. Loveless, Dure insisted that Mr. Houlihan come in for another interview right away. It was about 5:00 when he arrived. Kara showed him into Dure's office as she was leaving for the day.

"Since we last spoke," said Dure, "I have talked with our medical examiner. He tells me that the estimated time of death is from 9:00 in the morning on Friday through 5:00 Saturday afternoon. That is, as these cases go, a longish time interval, but it is apparently on account of the outdoor location and the disturbance of the remains by animals. But – and this is important in regards to proving your alibi – the most likely time of death is between noon and 3:00, either Friday or Saturday.

"Now you have told us that you left your house at 1:15 on Friday or thereabouts."

Houlihan nodded.

"And your wife was alive at that time?"

"Yes, sir. She was in the kitchen when I left."

"And you told this to the police?"

"Yes, sir."

"That being the case, we can narrow down the likely time of death to the time between 1:15 on Friday and 5:00 on Saturday, and the most likely time of death to between 1:15 and 3:00 on Friday and between noon and 3:00 on Saturday.

"What this means for us is that if we can establish that your wife was alive at 1:15 on Friday, and that you were away from home between 1:15 on Friday and 5:00 on Saturday, you'll be in the clear.

"Your testimony that she was alive at 1:15 counts for something, but obviously in the circumstances it would be good to have some corroborating evidence. So that's one question. What evidence can we get that would show your wife was alive at 1:15 on Friday – or even later?"

Houlihan slumped forward, as if he were frustrated by a clue in a crossword puzzle. "Maybe she talked with someone on her phone," he suggested. "There would be a record of that, right?"

"There would be . . . on her phone and on the phone of whomever she talked with. Do you know where her phone is?"

Houlihan shook his head.

"Do you know with whom she might have talked?"

Houlihan shook his head. "I keep away from that. I don't want to know."

Dure looked long at Houlihan. "We'll work on the phone angle," he said at last. "Anything else?"

"Not unless maybe a neighbor saw her outside."

Dure nodded. "Okay," he said, "The other question is: what evidence can we produce to corroborate that you were away from home from 1:15 on? Do you have receipts? Gas station receipts with date and time? Restaurant receipts?"

"I don't have any receipts," said Houlihan. His voice was loud.

"But you would need receipts for tax purposes, your trip being for your business?" said Dure.

"I just use the standard mileage rate for my truck and I don't bother to keep track of meals. Its not a big expense, and my accountant tells me they're only half deductible anyway, and they can trigger an audit. So I stay away from it."

Dure did not show any surprise or alarm at these answers.

"It's a cash business," volunteered Houlihan, as if that explained matters.

"Do you ever use credit cards?" asked Dure

"My . . . wife has . . . or had, one, more than one, and I have a – what do you call it? – companion card, through her. I use it sometimes."

"Did you happen to use it on this trip we are talking about?"

"Since it's a cash business, I usually take care of all the, you know, little expenses with cash."

"Do I then conclude, that for the whole of the weekend, you do not have a single receipt?"

"My truck has a four-door cab. I have the back rigged up so I can sleep there. For just a two-day outing, I don't need to shower, so I save the hotel cost."

"Do you keep a mileage log?"

"Yes, I use it for the standard mileage allowance."

"Alright," said Dure "Let us consider. What proof can we show that you were at this gun show during the time that your wife was killed?"

"Now that I think about it, I did pay one thing with my credit card. I had to pay a vendor's fee to the promoter, and I did that on-line with my credit card."

"That is something. How much was the fee?"

"Seventy-five dollars for an outdoor space in the parking area."

"Not a major expense?" said Dure

"No, sir."

"You wouldn't consider that it would break your bank if you blew off the show and wasted the fee?"

Houlihan laughed and winced and gave a shy smile as if he were being forced to admit something nice about himself. "No, not that," he said, shaking his head.

"Did you pack your meals, or did you buy them while you were out?"

"I used to pack them when I first started out. I did. But now I mostly just go to some other vendors at the show. I get the stuff early and keep it in my cart so I don't have to close up to go eat."

"Could you get the people from whom you bought your food to testify that, yes, on such-and-such a date, at such-and-such a time, this man came to my wagon and bought such-and-so?" said Dure

Houlihan adjusted himself in his seat. "Maybe I could," he said. "*If* they could remember. *If* I could find them. I don't know." He shook his head in doubt. "I remember what I had and I remember the location of the wagons in relation to where I had my trailer, but I don't . . . can't right at the moment remember the names of them."

"Can you get a list of food vendors from the promoter?"

"Probably can."

"Do that. If you have success in finding a witness, call me. We'll work up an affidavit to memorialize the testimony. Do you ever get headaches?"

"I do get bad migraines sometimes."

"Do you get headaches when you're out of town with your shave-ice cart?"

Houlihan bent forward, to his left, and put his hand to his chin, appearing thoughtful. "I can't remember any . . . don't know," he said.

"How did you and your wife get along?"

Houlihan shrugged. "Fine. No problems."

"Arguments?" said Dure

"Rarely. Probably the same or less than most people."

"Any physical violence?"

"No." Houlihan drew the word out, making it sound as if the suggestion were absurd. His face wore a sad expression.

"If the prosecution checks the Family Court for any cases or orders involving you or your wife, will they find anything?"

"No, nothing of that sort at all. My wife and I got along fine."

Dure jotted a note. "You've got your assignment," he said.

Houlihan nodded.

"While you're doing that, don't talk to anyone about the case. You just find and identify people who can say where you were when – we'll get their affidavits. Got it?"

"Yes, sir," said Houlihan.

4.

The next morning, Dure called Kara into his office. "I think we should talk to young Houlihan. The testimonies of Houlihan and his neighbor don't agree at all points. Maybe the son can throw some light on the discrepancies. Call him and have him come in here, would you?"

Kara was a perceptive and intelligent woman, and she knew her boss. Adding up his words and his tone of voice and his body language, she knew that what Dure meant was "Get him in here right away." So that's what she did. She used her secretary's magic, in this case, a vague implication that the lawyer needed to see him about something so important that not even she was allowed to know what it was. She got him to agree to come in at 10:30.

At 10:43 a young man came into the office. It was Liam Houlihan. "Please take a seat, Mr. Houlihan," said Kara. "I'll let Mr. Dure know that you're here." She took him to be a body builder. His upper body was an agglomeration of enormous slabs of muscle, and veins stood in high relief on his bare arms. His face was florid and acned, and yet, when he flashed one quick smile, it was sweet and innocent.

He stepped over into the waiting area but did not sit down. While Kara used the phone with Dure, Liam Houlihan stood bouncing on his toes, turning this way and that, and periodically smacking the palm of his left hand with his balled-up right fist.

Kara led him to Dure's office, then took a seat off to the side.

Liam Houlihan sat in front of Dure's desk, pressing his thighs with his straight arms so as to arch his back. Dure, with his head bent forward and his eyes rolled up in their sockets, eyebrows raised, was watching him closely.

Dure went through the usual amenities, offered his sympathy for the loss, gave Liam a little legal background, which probably went over his head, about Dure's representation of Liam's father. Then he began to dig in.

"I take it you've talked to the police, or they've talked to you?"

"Yeah." Young Houlihan exhaled the word short and sharp.

"Let's start there. What did they ask you and what did you say?"

Liam leaned back in his chair and rotated his head in a circle, then began to speak. "Who'd wanna hurt my mom? What'd I know about it? Where was I? Where was my dad? Who are the neighbors? Stuff."

"Tell me what you told the police . . . and, anything you might additionally have remembered since you spoke with the police."

"I didn't know anybody who would want to hurt my mom. I didn't know anything about what happened. My dad didn't do it and neither did I. The neighbors are who they are."

"This is what you told the police?"

"Yeah."

"In those exact words?"

The young man snorted.

"There is no law that says you have to help your father," said Dure.

A period of silence ensued as a battle of stares took place. There was no way that a young kid could prevail against the intense stare of Dure's light colored hazel eyes, glowing out of the dark caverns that were his eye sockets. Young Houlihan's hands were grasping the arm rests of the chair in which he sat; he twisted his grip outwards, as if he were trying to twist off the upholstery. "Okay," he said.

Dure nodded, and the young man began to speak.

"I didn't have to work Friday – that's the first day they asked about – so I slept in. I got up around nine. My apartment mate, Matt, was gone already. I ate breakfast, checked my e-mail, surfed the internet. Then I went out driving around, had lunch around 1:30 at Arby's, and got back around three. It was a recovery day, so I didn't work out. I did a load of clothes, spent some time on Facebook, checked e-mail again. I made dinner, streamed a movie, checked my e-mail, surfed some more and went to bed."

Kara was taking notes on a steno pad.

"And Saturday?" said Dure.

The young man gave another similar recitation, including things that he likely would not have included but for the fact that he had been asked for details on a previous occasion. For example, the fact that he hadn't taken a shower in the morning because he had to be at work early, but had taken a shower after his workout at the gym.

"Did you happen to visit your parents' house on either day?" asked Dure.

"No!" he said, as if daring Dure to make something of it.

"Is the job at the deli the only job you have?"

"Yeah."

"And it's part-time?"

"Yeah." Liam nodded.

"Where did this interview take place?"

"Two men came to my apartment Monday afternoon. They weren't wearing uniforms, but the one showed me ID."

"Do you remember their names?"

"No."

"How had your parents been getting along?"

"Good, I guess. No problem."

"How'd you get the cut on your arm?"

"My arm?"

"Yes, your right forearm, right there."

"Oh, that. That's not a cut, that's just a scratch."

"I see. How'd you get it?"

"How'd I get it?"

Dure nodded.

"I, uh, scratched it on a lettuce crate at work. They have these wires holding them together, and one of them scratched me."

"Did your parents always get along?"

Liam let his head sway back and forth briefly. Then he shrugged. "Yeah. Far as I knew."

"Did you ever hear – well, let me back up for a minute. How long had your mother been working at her job?"

"She worked at the library for a long time – long as I can remember. She got promoted to the head of everything about . . . I think six years ago?"

"Did you ever her her complain about any of her co-workers?"

The young man smiled. "She used to complain about some of the patrons. But that was a long time ago when she actually worked in the library." He was smiling as if he were recalling some fond memory; then became serious again. "But since I went to college? . . . I can't recall anything . . . oh, . . . yeah." He laughed again. "I don't know if you would call it complaining, but she used to talk about this idiot who worked there, Chauncey Blackwell, I remember his name. He was retarded or something, couldn't talk right."

"Did there seem to be any hostility on Mr. Blackwell's part?"

"Nah, it was just, like, you know, how stupid can somebody be?"

Quite suddenly the young man's eyes filled with water. He blinked vigorously and sniffed and threw his head back as if he were determined not to let any tear trickle down his face. He turned his head to look away from Dure.

The yellow legal pad in front of Dure had eight short notations of subjects for the questioning of Liam. Dure had made, during this interview, tick marks by four of them. However, instead of continuing on to the remaining four, he suddenly said, "Alright, Liam. Thank you for coming in." He stood.

The young man pushed down on the arm rests with his huge arms and his body came up from the chair is if propelled by a giant spring.

"Oh, one last thing," said Dure. "Have you ever taken anabolic steroids?"

Liam had started for the door, but stopped and turned. "Who, me?"

"Have you?"

Liam hesitated, his face a picture of perplexity. Suddenly it lit up with a bright smile. "I plead the fifth," he said. He turned quickly, bounced out the door and was gone.

Dure rubbed his chin. Kara finished writing, then left also. Dure got up and stepped across the hall into Ralph's office.

"Ralph, you're my one-man mock jury. Here's what I've got."

Ralph sat up straight. His large, round eyes were unblinking while he listened.

"So what do you think?" said Dure.

"Her old man did it. The husband."

"The apparent lack of motive doesn't bother you?"

"Naah, they were married," said Ralph. "Don't get me wrong. I love my wife. But some of 'em . . .."

"I'm trying out a line of defense. What would a jury say to this? You know the prosecution has to prove guilt beyond a reasonable doubt. So, what we have to do is raise a reasonable doubt. If the case gets to court, I might have to suggest to the jury that someone else did the crime."

"Right," said Ralph.

"Suppose I suggest to the jury that young Houlihan did it, not his father. What would a jury say?"

"Huh?" The idea was too new to Ralph. He couldn't grasp it right away.

"Would a jury find that there was reasonable doubt that the father did it if we suggest that the son might be the one who had done it?"

"The kid? . . . I don't know."

"Isn't there such a thing as 'roid rage,' you know, aggressive or violent behavior due to taking anabolic steroids?"

"Yeah."

"Did you see the kid? He looks like he might be susceptible to that."

"Sceptible?"

"Like he might get 'roid rage?"

"I heard of that. I don't know."

"If it comes to that, I am prepared to suggest it. But I can't suggest he might be the one if I know for sure that he did not do it. On the other hand, if I knew that he did it, putting suspicion on him could get him prosecuted. And, I would be ill-serving Mr. Houlihan to send his son to the electric chair. So I do not want to know either that he did it, nor that he did not do it. So I cut my questioning short. It is the government's business to find out the guilty party, not ours."

* * *

Late Friday morning, Ralph was working on another case, entering medical damages into a spreadsheet. His thick, clumsy fingers first typed in a short text, using the "hunt and bash" method. Swiveling his head to the right, he looked at the paper he was working from, looked down at the 10-key numeric pad and bashed in a few digits. Then he looked up and strained forward to read the computer screen. He took a short, dull pencil from behind his right ear and made a check mark on the paper, pausing to get a good look at the next item he was to enter. He replaced the pencil behind his ear and prepared to bash in another entry.

A light tapping noise was on the door to his office. Dure was standing in the doorway. "Ralph, let's get out of the office," he said.

Without a word, Ralph simultaneously stood and closed up his work as if Dure had told him the building was on fire. When they were outside on the sidewalk, Dure said, "We're going to go to the Houlihans' house." Ralph nodded.

In the car a conversation of sorts took place. "It's exactly a week ago that the murder took place," said Dure, "according to the medical examiners. Either today, Friday, or tomorrow. My hunch is it happened on the Friday, so let's just go and observe the *locus in quo* . . . at the same time of the week."

Ralph responded with an inarticulate grunt.

They drove to Sunderly Chase and backed into the Houlihans' driveway. Their windows were rolled down on this warm June morning. The roar of lawn mowers, leaf blowers, and weed whackers resounded throughout the neighborhood. The roar reached them even from the next street, a quarter of a mile away. Through an open vista through the trees, one could see a mower going back and forth, the operator standing up on a platform on the back of the mower.

"Make a note," said Dure "to find out when Mr. Houlihan and these neighbors have their lawns cut, and who the mowers are."

To their right was the house of the Vanderlogens; to their left, Mr. Loveless. Across the street were the Sweets. Other than the distant lawn crews, no human being was to be seen. Of course, given the curvature of the street and the size of the lots, people could have been out in their back yards, and the occupants of Dure's car would have been unable to see them.

"You think one of the lawn crews did it?" said Ralph.

"One of the lawn crews?" said Dure. "Could be."

"Lotta Mexicans," said Ralph.

"That appears to be the case," said Dure. "What do you think the motive would have been?"

"Money," said Ralph, as if it had been a stupid question.

"The dead woman's purse was found in the house. Her billfold was in it. As far as anyone has been able to tell, nothing was missing from either the purse or the billfold. The police found a cell phone and a ring of keys on the body," said Dure.

Ralph thought this over for a moment. "That fits with what I said before . . . the husband did it."

The two men sat for a while without talking. Ralph became fidgety, as if he were a seven-year-old boy forced to sit still in class. Dure, however, quietly observed the surroundings. After a time, he said, "I believe I saw movement through the picture window in the house across the street. Let's go see if we can talk with . . . the Sweets, I think live there." The two men got out of the car and walked down and across the empty street to the driveway of the Sweets' house. Going to the door, Dure pressed the doorbell button.

The door swung open. "Yes?" said Mrs. Sweet. She supported herself with one arm against the door jamb while with the other held the storm door open a few inches. She acted as if she did not recognize them, although they had spoken briefly to her before, when she had told them to come back when her husband was home.

"Good morning, ma'am," said Dure "We don't want to come in, but we would like to speak briefly with you about the happenings, the unfortunate happening, at the Houlihans."

The crack in the door began to close.

Dure let it close all the way. With the large pane of glass between him and Mrs. Sweet, he said, loudly, "She was no friend of yours I take it?"

The door opened a crack. "No. She wasn't." And the door shut again.

"Do you dislike Mr. Houlihan, too?" yelled Dure.

Open. "No." Close.

"Well, he needs help."

Open. "What can I do?" It was not an offer of help, but an expression of inability. Close.

Ralph rubbed the short hair on the top of his head with his palm and looked away from the door. He sighed.

Dure yelled, "You can help me find out what happened and I'm going to go hoarse in a minute."

The door opened again, wider than before. "I told the police everything I know. That's all I can do, right?" The door stayed part way open.

"Not at all," said Dure. He spoke rapidly. "You might have remembered something since. The police might have missed something. I may know something that the police don't that would match up with something you observed." He paused. "Please, okay?" he said.

"Alright," she said. "What?"

"Thank you," said Dure. And they began to talk.

In response to the question whether she knew of anyone who might have any animosity against Mrs. Houlihan, she could think of no one; but when Dure asked her what Mrs. Houlihan was like, Mrs. Sweet said she was a terror. Because Mrs. Houlihan worked for the county, she knew just which person to call to bring down the county on anybody who violated any county ordinance, such as letting the lawn grass get too high, or open burning out of season. And she did the same thing with the development's homeowners' association. If anybody put a sign in their yard, or left their garbage canisters too long at the curb, Tiffany was on the phone to the head of the homeowners' association. And maybe on account of Tiffany's relentless calling down authority on others, their own property had to be faultless, to the point where her poor husband Howard had to hire a lawn maintenance company to keep his wife off his back, even though he didn't work a regular job and probably could have done the yard work himself.

On whom, in particular, had Mrs. Houlihan "called down authority"? Just about everybody in the neighborhood at one time or another. She had even made a complaint about the Sweets' putting a political sign in their yard one year. That's how they found out that the rules of the homeowners' association forbade it.

Mrs. Sweet came out of the house and stood on the porch with them. Had she seen anything unusual that Friday or Saturday? Of course she did not stand around at the picture window and watch the neighbors all the time, and she couldn't say she had paid any attention to the Houlihans' house those days more than any others. But she had seen, around lunchtime on Friday – she had told the police this – she was going out to check the mail and had seen a small red sports car backing out of the Houlihans' driveway and zooming away. She pointed to the place. She couldn't say the make or model, she wasn't a car expert. She hadn't paid attention to the driver, it was a man she thought.

Dure asked: "What can you tell us about the neighbors on the other side of the Houlihans? The Vanderlogens, is it?"

"Yes. Right. They're, um . . . they're okay. I don't know too much about them. Mr. Vanderlogen is like, really tall, like professional basketball player tall. But you know, husband, wife, two kids. Just normal."

A pick-up truck towing a trailer full of lawn maintenance equipment came down the street and stopped in front of the Sweets' house. Men got out and unhooked the gate at the back of the trailer that also served as a loading ramp. An enormous roar began, and a huge mower slowly rolled down the ramp. Mrs. Sweet seemed anxious to get back into her house.

Yelling thanks to her over the noise and giving her a wave, Dure turned to go. He checked his phone. To Ralph he said, "It's 12:35. Let's go have lunch."

* * *

There no longer seemed to be urgency about the Houlihan case. Mr. Houlihan himself was off chasing the promoter of the gun show for a list of food vendors, trying to locate the ones he had bought food from, and presumably finding the persons with whom he dealt who could testify as to his whereabouts at the time of the murder of his wife.

A week passed. Then came a piece of startling news that unsettled the case.

The Essex County Courthouse in downtown Canterbury had been until 2007 a small, handsome Greek Revival building with four large marble columns in its front. It was "rehabilitated" into an enormous, brick and glass building taking up half a block and called the Justice Complex of Essex County. The facade of the old courthouse was retained and makes up a small part of the front of the new building. The marble columns, however, instead of their former imposing appearance, now appear insignificant in the overwhelming height and width of the new building. The incongruity of the small Greek Revival facade embedded in the predominating modernist front gives the building the appearance of an architectural joke.

Friday afternoon, gray-visaged Dure with his shrewd hazel eyes was sitting in the cafeteria of the Justice Complex, which was in the basement, negotiating a plea bargain with a junior prosecutor. A television monitor was mounted on the wall not too far away, blaring news from the Vulpex News Service. This noise meant that their conversation was private, because the din from the television drowned out their words to anyone more that a few feet away.

"You want to try this case?" said Dure. The tone and lilt of his voice made the sentence mean: Are you really sure you want to do something so foolish as to take this case to trial?

The prosecutrix, a Ms. Wallace, was a woman in her late twenties with a long neck and long, wavy brown hair. "Yeah. Yeah, I want to put this guy away."

Dure's dour expression did not change. He stared off past her into the distance for a long moment. "So far," he said, "he has refrained from filing a criminal complaint against her. If she continues to press, he may change his mind."

Ms. Wallace's upper body swung back and forth slightly, like an inverted pendulum.

Dure continued, "The guy is sitting at the dinner table. She, in an unprovoked attack, smashes a wooden chair over his head. When he recovers, he picks her up and heaves her bodily out the window – a first floor window, she only fell about four feet into some bushes. They both had to go to the hospital. As far as I can tell, they don't want a divorce, although if you press this matter, you may cause a divorce. As I said, he could press charges against her as well."

"So . . .?"

"So . . . reduce the charges to a misdemeanor. That'll send the case from Superior Court to the Family Court. That'll get the case off both our desks – and it's a Family Court matter anyway."

"Then, according to you, your guy could still file felony charges against the wife."

"We could come to some agreement about that."

The prosecutrix said nothing for a moment. On the television, an advertisement concluded and local headlines came on. "Essex County police are investigating another beheading," said the news anchor. "According to police spokesman, a woman was discovered in her driveway, decapitated, at around 6:30 this morning. Melinda Erdody has more on the story." The picture changed to that of a reporter holding a microphone in a suburban development. "John, I'm here in a development called Hickory Heights in front of the house where a woman's decapitated body was discovered early this morning." Behind the reporter, a typical two-story suburban house could be seen with police tape surrounding it. "I've been talking with Carole Quentin who is the neighbor who discovered the body and alerted the police. What did you see this morning?" The reporter pushed the microphone in the face of a middle-aged woman. "We're just all in shock," said the woman. "I was out walking the dog and I saw this body lying in the driveway. And Shatzi – that's my dog – was tugging on her leash and pulled me over there. I saw . . . oh, it was just too horrible, and I immediately backed away. I had my cell phone and called 911."

Ms. Wallace was saying something. Dure interrupted her. "Rather than risk putting two people in jail with felony convictions," he said, "and causing a divorce, it might make sense to let the Family Court sort it out." He slapped the table with the flat of his hand and stood up. "Let me know soon," he said. He nodded to Ms. Wallace and walked to the stairwell and went up to the first floor and went out of the Justice Complex.

Once outside he called his regular investigator. "Kurt? . . . Yeah. I want you to find out what you can about a murder that happened this morning. . . . Yeah, in Hickory Heights, victim a woman. Canterbury Police are investigating. . . . Okay, thanks."

5.

Tuesday morning at 9:18 Kara answered the telephone. After speaking briefly to the caller, she put him on hold and called Dure on the intercom. "Walter, Rod Preston would like to speak with you."

Two minutes later, Dure crossed the hall and leaned into Ralph's office. "Ralph, we have to go down to the police station."

Ralph's wide, round eyes asked why.

"Houlihan's under arrest," said Dure, "and charged with the murder of his wife."

At the police station, the duty officer knew Dure. He asked what Houlihan had been charged with.

"Murder first degree," said the officer.

"Anything else?" he asked.

"Not at this time. You know how the system works," answered the officer gruffly.

Ralph was offended at the lack of deference shown to Dure. To get to see their client, they had to go through the same rigmarole as anyone else.

After a long wait, a police officer led them to an interview room in which they had already put Houlihan. There was a small, plain, gray metal table with no drawers and three cheap chairs with molded plastic seats. On one wall was what looked like a one-way mirror. The flooring was of aged and discolored linoleum tiles. Several semi-circular dents were in the floor as if something heavy had been dropped.

Houlihan had stood up when they entered. He was wearing the same kind of faded jeans – except without a belt -- and worn flannel shirt as he had worn to the initial interview in Dure's office. They might even have been the exact same clothes. His head jutted forward perhaps more than the last time they had seen him and his face expressed anxiety; but the hint of a smile kept flickering on and off his face, like a light bulb with a loose connection. The officer left and they sat.

"They're not supposed to monitor attorney conversations," said Dure, "but let's assume that they are. So, don't tell me anything that would be incriminating. Keeping that in mind, tell me what happened."

"I signed a confession," said Houlihan.

Dure said nothing right away, but stared with his glowing eyes at Houlihan. Under this glare, Houlihan dropped his gaze as if he were a teenager who was disappointed to find that his clever joke has not gone over well with the adult on whom he had tried it out.

"You will please to recall that I advised you not to discuss the case with anyone," said Dure at last.

"Yes, sir." Mr. Houlihan gave up the point easily.

"That included especially the police," said Dure

Houlihan nodded, hope fading from his eyes.

After a long moment of silence, Dure said "Why?"

"They were going to charge Liam. I'm old anyway. It doesn't matter that much."

"But you didn't think Liam had done it?"

"No. No, sir."

"But you thought they would be able to convict him, even though he hadn't done it?" said Dure

Houlihan began to talk volubly, rationalizing what he had done, and as he talked, he pursued his thought until apparently even he recognized that his reasoning was weak. He kept circling back to his starting point until he finally wound down, like a top running out of momentum. Dure began to question him in an orderly fashion. telling him to keep his voice down.

He had been driving back to Canterbury from his expedition to gather witnesses for his alibi, *as Dure had instructed him to do.* (It almost seemed like he was setting up a rationale to blame Dure for what had happened.) He was on eastbound Route 22, just a couple of miles from home, when his truck ran into a ditch. (How did that happen? Houlihan didn't know, wasn't sure.) The police came. One of the investigating officers had been at Houlihans' house in a peripheral role during the investigation of his wife's death. He recognized Houlihan and struck up a friendly conversation. After a bit, the officer steered the conversation onto the topic of the death of Houlihan's wife, then suggested, in a friendly way, "Whyn't you come down to the station with me. You could clear up a couple of things, maybe help us to solve this case . . . find out who murdered your wife. You want us to find that out, right?"

So Houlihan rode with the officer to the police station while his truck was towed away. At the station they had questioned him about his son, did he know his son's whereabouts at the time the murder was committed? Wasn't it true, as the neighbors had informed the police, that his son did not get along with his parents, especially his mother? There had been shouting matches; wasn't his son bitter? Hadn't he moved out of the house?

How do you know that he didn't do it? the police had asked over and over. You weren't with him at the time. Gradually they built in an insinuation that the only way he could be sure that his son didn't do it was that he knew that someone else did it.

They showed him a paper which they claimed was an arrest warrant for his son. They wanted to be sure, however, before they arrested him, and to be fair, they were checking with the father to make sure they weren't making a mistake. It was all a matter of getting to the truth and shielding the innocent.

The interview went on for hours, with two different detectives coming in and out of the room. They asked him about life insurance and he told them of a $750K policy on his wife, but Houlihan stressed that he was the beneficiary, not his son.

They went over the facts of the crime, the lack of any motive for anyone else, the lack of any sightings of a stranger, and finally made it look like there were only two possible suspects, Houlihan or his son. If it's not you, they said, then it must be your son. It has to be one or the other. "A red sports car was observed leaving the scene on Friday. Your son drives a red sports car doesn't he?"

The one detective was sympathetic. Domestic violence happens, he said. They see it all the time. I mean, some of these women deserve it. There could be justification and mitigation. So he drew out from Houlihan some episodes where his wife had been cruel and actually violent. See, said the detective, you're not the first. You know how those women get off from murder charges by claiming domestic violence? That can work both ways. Probably a judge would be sympathetic, but only if you come clean and admit the truth.

If Houlihan would admit the truth, he could clear his conscience, it would be taken into account favorably by the court, it would put his son in the clear, the police would respect his honesty, do what they could for him.

The charges could be plea-bargained down to manslaughter. Houlihan began to consider the idea.

The other detective previewed what a trial would look like, the publicity that probably would result, the kind of evidence the prosecution could put on, the severity of the court against defendants who stubbornly refuse to admit their crime and show remorse.

Finally, said Houlihan, it made sense just to end the matter, get it over with. So he agreed that he had done it. His primary motivation was to protect his son. He figured he could explain to his son that he hadn't really done it and why he had confessed.

He thought that when he agreed, that would be the end of the questioning, but it wasn't. First, he had to repeat his admission in front of both detectives. Then they began to question him about the physical evidence and ask him how he had actually carried out the killing. Houlihan just agreed to whatever was plausible, because at that point, he just wanted to get it over with. They wanted to know where the head was. Houlihan said he didn't know, which really caused the one detective to go ballistic and the other to act most concerned. This occasioned another long session of questioning, at the end of which Houlihan said only that he couldn't remember.

The detectives weren't happy with that either, so they kept at him. Finally, just to get to the end, so Houlihan claimed, he said he had put it in a black plastic trash bag and taken it to the county landfill. It was too late to do it on Friday, he said, so he did it Saturday morning.

The police were satisfied with this and put together a statement. They got a videographer in the room. But now Houlihan balked at the black plastic bag business, and ironically, the police were now tired and worn out.

Just to get the confession signed, they took that part out. Houlihan read the statement in the presence of the two detectives and the videographer.

When it was all over, they let him make a phone call, which was when he had called Dure.

At the end of Houlihan's story, Dure stood up, but did not make as if to leave. "Do you want me to defend you?" he asked.

"I've signed a confession. Doesn't that mean it's all over?"

"Not necessarily. . . . Did you murder your wife?"

"No, but I guess I did now." said Houlihan.

"What does that mean?"

"I mean I said I did it. You can't take that back, can you?"

Dure made a grimace and looked away from Houlihan. After a moment he turned again to him and said, "Long story short, the prosecution has to prove its case. If you did not in fact murder your wife, there is a chance that we can prevent that proof, even against your confession."

"Then I didn't do it."

Dure regarded him closely. "I don't know whether I should keep you as a client or not. You don't follow my advice."

Houlihan was staring at the floor with a deep frown on his mouth. His jaw quivered.

"You know the judge still could give you the death penalty. Even with ten years of appeals, you'd still be only, what? sixty?"

"Sixty-one," said Houlihan. He put his face in his hands. After a moment, he sat up. "I didn't think," said Houlihan. "I was tired, confused. I wanted to protect my son."

Dure turned away and walked to the door of the little room. He put his hand on the door knob, paused, and turned back to look at Houlihan. "It is exceedingly difficult to help clients who ignore my advice."

"No," said Houlihan. "I want you to represent me."

"Would you like time to think it over?" said Dure "I can go away and come back later."

"Don't be so harsh. I made a mistake. Don't abandon me."

Dure came back from the door. They talked for some time about things not directly related to the case. Probably Houlihan did not recognize that Dure was testing him, trying to make sure that he knew his man. Dure did not want to take on a hard case if it was going to be a situation of his being exploited by a lying client.

Before leaving Houlihan, Dure said, "Do NOT talk to anyone about this case. Even though you are in jail and even though you have signed a confession, DO NOT TALK with anyone. That includes any cellmate you may have. At this point, your case is not entirely lost, although it is a hell of a lot rougher than it was, but if you go blabbing any more, it may put the case so far behind the eight ball that nothing can be done. Do you understand me?"

"Yes, sir."

"Good. KEEP YOUR MOUTH SHUT!"

As Ralph was driving Dure back to the office, he wanted to discuss the case, even though Dure seemed thoughtful, or glum, or brooding.

"You really think he's innocent?" began Ralph.

It took a moment for Dure to respond. "I don't know," he said. "There is evidence from which one could conclude that he murdered his wife."

"So, what's the point of defending him?"

Dure gave Ralph a look. "In the first place, he did not actually murder his wife unless a jury says he did. In the second place, it is necessary to preserve our liberties that the government be made to prove a defendant's guilt beyond a reasonable doubt. In the third place, even if he is convicted, the matter of penalty will be an important contested issue. And lastly, without representation, he will sit in jail, whereas if I can get him out on bail, he could help prepare his defense."

Ralph did not have an answer to any of this, so he launched into his theory of the case. They were sitting at a light. "I was thinking myself," he said, "that it might have been either Houlihan or his son. I mean, who else had a motive?"

Dure said, "The only way to win this case now will be a successful Motion to Suppress the confession. If the confession stays in the case, it will no longer be sufficient for us to merely make the government prove its case. The confession will do that. We would have to prove that someone else did it, which right now looks like a tall order."

"And neither of them has a good alibi," said Ralph.

6.

At home after work, while his dinner was heating up in the microwave, Dure drank a beer and read the news on an i-pad. He habitually drank one can of beer when he got home. He poured the beer into a Pilsner glass, let the head develop, then tapped in a few grains of salt, pensively observing the grains fall to the bottom of the glass, trailing bubbles.

Unmarried Dure lived by himself in a 2,300 square foot condominium which he kept as uncluttered, clean, and orderly as a Marine Corps barracks. One of the bedrooms he used for sleeping, and the other was an office where he could work at home.

After dinner that evening, he listened to recordings of Beethoven's late string quartets (he listened to the Cavatina of Opus 130 twice) until eleven o'clock, when he went to bed.

The alarm on his bedside clock was set for 6:00, but almost never did it go off. He would wake a few minutes before six and turn it off before it sounded. On this morning, he woke a little earlier than usual, around 5:20. As often happened, his "sleep" had been restless. He got out of bed and padded to the work desk in the other room. He began writing down ideas on a yellow legal pad for his Motion to Suppress, and noted the evidence he would like to have in support, if it could be obtained.

After showering, he mechanically ate breakfast, while keeping his yellow pad next to his plate and jotting ideas as they occurred to him.

At the office, mid-morning, Liam Houlihan, accompanied by Ralph, came in with two large department store shopping bags – full of cash. They went into Dure's little conference room and dumped one bag out on the conference table. It appeared that all the bills were twenties. It took most of an hour to count and re-count fifty stacks of 100 bills each.

When the hundred thousand dollars had been counted out from the first bag, a sizable pile still remained, probably about a fifth of the size of the initial pile. That would equate to some twenty to thirty thousand more dollars, plus what was in the other shopping bag.

Ralph picked up the phone in the conference room and dialed Dure's extension. "It's all ready," he said.

Dure brought in a receipt which he signed and gave to Liam, and a briefcase, into which Ralph put the stacks as he bound them with rubber bands.

Dure sat in a chair in the corner of the room. "This will take a little thought," he said. Addressing Ralph, he said, "You will obviously deposit the fee, but as to what Liam should do" – he turned to Liam – "if things go well in court this afternoon, you may want the cash to post bail . . . and we don't yet know the exact amount. If you deposit the money in the bank, you may not be able to get it out again today. If you buy a cashier's check, we don't know the amount . . . Here's what I suggest: How much do you have?" he asked.

"I don't know," said Liam.

Ralph put in, "If the two shopping bags held the same amount, then the first one had about a hundred and twenty or a hundred and thirty thousand. So if you add the twenty or thirty remainder from the first bag to the hundred twenty or so from the second bag, that would make roughly a hundred forty or a hundred and fifty thousand."

"I suggest," said Dure, "that you buy two cashier's checks for fifty thousand each, payable to Clerk of Court, and keep the rest in cash. That way, if bail is set at anything less than a hundred and fifty, you can post it today. If the court refuses bail, you can deposit the checks."

Ralph and Liam left to go to the bank.

Later, Ralph told Dure what he had observed when Liam Houlihan had retrieved the cash:

They had gone to a self-storage locker, Liam having asked Ralph to go with him for safety on account of a large amount of cash. Liam had unlocked the combination lock on unit #121, thrown up the overhead door, and gone in. Ralph stood just outside and watched. The unit was not full. Along one wall were what seemed to be some old equipment from the shave-ice business; along the other was a row of black plastic trash bags of vague and lumpy shapes. Liam walked down the narrow aisle between the trash bags and the equipment to a filing cabinet at the rear of the unit. He opened the drawer second from the bottom and drew out a paper shopping bag of some kind. "Whoa!" he had exclaimed. He put the bag down while he opened the bottom drawer. From there he took another, similar bag. "Whoa, momma!" he exclaimed again.

He kicked the front of the bottom drawer. It slammed shut with a hollow metallic clang. A pile of junk on top of the filing cabinet shifted, and some of it fell down. Liam cursed and bent to pick up what had fallen. It looked, in the dim light at the back of the unit, like a large hunting knife in a leather sheath.

* * *

Dure was standing in the middle of his office, head bent forward, rubbing his chin with thumb and forefinger. In a few minutes he would leave to go to court for the arraignment of Houlihan. Externally, he was ready. He had the necessary papers in his briefcase, and his argument for bail outlined. His dark suit was without spot or wrinkle and his black wingtip shoes gleamed. As a busy lawyer, he had given up the time-consuming practice of spit-shining his shoes; nevertheless, his shoes were always shinier than any civilian's.

Coming out of his reverie, he took a deep breath, and grabbed the handle of his briefcase. As he strode away from his desk, the briefcase slid off the desk, swung down, and banged against his leg.

The small courtroom was dingy and dim. The judge was doing arraignments via a video hook-up to the jail, so that the state would not have to transport prisoners to the courtroom. Dure, Ralph, and Liam Houlihan were sitting in the small set of benches for spectators at the back of the courtroom.

Judge Ozma was a young woman with short hair. The left half of her head was bleached blonde, and the right half was a natural-looking dark color. On the blonde half, there was about an inch and a half of dark roots growing out. She wore earrings of large, dangling hoops, and had nails painted lime green.

After what seemed a long time the bailiff called out "Commonwealth vs. Houlihan." Dure got up and went into the well of the court. "Good afternoon, Your Honor," he said, smiling. "Walter Dure for the defendant."

"Good afternoon, counselor. Bailiff, read the charges."

The bailiff read out a charge of first-degree murder. "Did the defendant hear that?" asked the judge.

A screen mounted to the side of the courtroom showed an image of Mr. Houlihan. The identical image appeared on a smaller screen at the counsel table where Dure sat, and presumably on the screen on the judge's small bench. Houlihan was dressed in orange fatigues and looked unhappy and unshaven. But he spoke loudly and clearly. "Yes, sir," he said.

"That's Ma'am," said the judge.

"Oh! Yes, ma'am," said Houlihan. "Sorry, judge, ma'am."

"That's all right," said the judge. "How does your client plead, Mr. . . . . Dure?"

"Not guilty, Your Honor."

"The clerk will enter a plea of not guilty. A scheduling order will be mailed to you."

"Thank you, Your Honor," said Dure

"Commonwealth vs. Jackson," said the judge.

"Your Honor," said Dure standing, "There's the matter of bail."

"Counsel, it's a first degree murder charge," said the judge.

"The defendant is still entitled to reasonable bail," said Dure.

"If you want to make an argument, I'll hear you, but I don't have all day. I still have – what?" the judge flipped through a pile of folders on the bench "another six or so arraignments to get through. So make it quick."

"May it please the court . . .." began Dure. He said a few words about Mr. Houlihan and some case law and –

The judge interrupted him. "Counselor, do you have more to add?"

"I do, Your Honor," said Dure.

"Be quick," said the judge.

"Thank you, Your Honor. As Your Honor will recall . . .." Dure continued his argument.

The judge interrupted him again. "Bail will be set at 500 thousand dollars cash bail. Thank you for your argument, counselor Commonwealth vs. Jackson," said the judge.

* * *

In *Brady v. Maryland,* the U.S. Supreme Court ruled that suppression by the prosecution of evidence favorable to a defendant who has requested it violates due process. A "Brady letter," therefore, is a request by a defendant to the prosecution for any evidence that would be favorable to the defendant's case. Dure got a copy of his standard Brady letter, marked it up with the case name, case number, etc., changed the facts so that it would apply to the Houlihan case, and gave it to Kara to word process. When the revised draft came back to him, he added this paragraph:

> Since it appears that Mr. Houlihan's confession was coerced, Brady materials the prosecution is obligated to provide to the defense specifically include the confession itself, and all detective notes from the interrogation which led to the preparation of the statement signed by Mr. Houlihan while in police custody.

Then, as it was late Wednesday afternoon, he had Ralph in to discuss in a relaxed way the various (actually very few) cases in the office. This was one of the ways Dure did his thinking. He would bounce ideas off Ralph. It didn't really seem to matter whether Ralph had anything useful to say or not. About the Houlihan case, the discussion was brief.

"It seems," said Dure, with a sigh of annoyance, "that our friend must sit in jail for a while."

Ralph nodded. "I'm really starting to get a bad feeling about Mr. Houlihan. Right? He comes to you for defense, before he was arrested, right? From what Mr. Loveless said, he had motive, and his alibi was always kinda sketchy – and now he's confessed? I mean, you're the lawyer, but I wouldn't defend him. I always laid my courses level and plumb."

"Things are not always what they seem," said Dure.

* * *

Dure's office was a three-story building on the corner of Court and Milton Streets, across from the Justice Complex. It had been a two-story private residence to which a third floor had been added; it had been joined with the house next door by knocking out doorways in their common wall and the resulting building converted into apartments. Later, the building had been converted into commercial offices. The floors creaked and the level of the floors between the two buildings was uneven. Dure occupied the whole ground floor of the left side of the building. The first floor of the right side was occupied by Kurt Kniffe and Associates, Private Investigators.

At Dure's telephonically communicated request, Kurt Kniffe had stepped over to Dure's office. Kniffe (the K is pronounced) stood five feet, nine inches. He had thinning hair, but was not bald. He was wearing an inexpensive, nondescript gray suit. His was a plain, average face. He had a bland personality, but was ruthless when he needed to be. If he had grown up in

East Germany, he would have been an excellent STASI operative.

"The beheading in Hickory Heights," said Kniffe, speaking in a level, dispassionate tone, "appears to have been done by one Achmed al-Metoosi. The police have him in custody. It appears that Mr. al-Metoosi took offense at something his neighbor said about Mohammad. When she went out to walk her dog at around 6:00 a.m., he attacked and killed her. By the way, he killed the dog, too."

"Could this al-Metoosi also have murdered Mrs. Houlihan?" asked Dure.

"On current information, the answer is indeterminate, the proverbial six of one, half-dozen of the other. One factor to note is that al-Metoosi left the head where it fell. This would seem to indicate a variance in MO compared with the Houlihan case."

"I want you to look into a few things for me. One, check Mrs. Houlihan's social media accounts. I'll try to get any passwords from my client. Two, can you see if the police have questioned this al-Metoosi about the Houlihan case. Three, look into any enemies Mrs. Houlihan might have had. I find myself in the position of having to prove that someone other than my client murdered the woman."

Kniffe had taken notes in a small, top-bound notebook. To confirm his understanding, he recited his assignments back to Dure. He gave a last look at the small, neat script in which he had written his notes, then closed the notebook and replaced it in the inside pocket of his suit jacket. He nodded to Dure as he rose from the chair and silently left the office.

* * *

Dure made time to interview Houlihan again. Interviewing an inmate is not like interviewing a private citizen. There's so much wasted time: the prison bureaucracy makes the visitor wait and wait. Accordingly, to make use of his time, Dure had taken with him the as-yet slender file on the Houlihan case.

No matter what materials a prison waiting room is made of, whether linoleum, plaster, concrete, cinder block, wood, etc., and no matter how often it is cleaned, it always appears somehow greasy and grimy, dirty and dingy. Dure sat on an inexpensive, scoop-shaped plastic chair turning over the sheets of paper in the file which he held on his lap.

There were the notes of his initial interview. Buzzards in the backyard. His call to Preston; his call to Dr. Mulvaney. Houlihan's initial story, left home Friday at 1:15. A copy of his letter to Preston. The retainer agreement. More notes: his interview with Loveless. Dr. Mulvaney's report. Notes from his interview with Nan Shuettler, Mrs. Sweet. Houlihan again. Then Liam Houlihan. Coming to the end of the file, Dure flipped the pages back to the beginning and stoically began going through them again. Buzzards in the backyard. Buzzards in the backyard. Actually, they were vultures. Was Houlihan's inaccurate terminology the reason this little fact nagged at him?

"Mr. Dure, your client is in the interview room." A beefy guard with short hair and a very erect posture interrupted him. The guard had no smile, but a respectful manner.

The interview room was a large, open area where many family visits were taking place. Women and children were talking with inmates. There was an occasional smile, but most faces were glum. Dure and

Houlihan dragged two chairs apart to be away from the noise.

Houlihan did not look well. His scalp shone white for lack of sun, having been shorn of its shaggy, gray mane. "Starting to get scared?" said Dure. Houlihan looked at him with defeated eyes. "Being locked up is not so bad," he said. "It's the other inmates that make it hard."

For his forty-five minutes of waiting and his forty-five minute interview, this is what Dure got:

The list of vendors which Houlihan got from the sponsor of the gun show was in his pick-up truck. Houlihan had marked a few vendors which had been located near his trailer and which he remembered. He thought they would remember him. Presumably his truck had been taken to a repair shop after the crash. Houlihan asked Dure to check on it.

His wife's circle of acquaintance would have to be her co-workers and her political friends. The Houlihans did not belong to any church or clubs.

"Did you notice anything suspicious or out of the ordinary in the weeks preceding the murder?" Dure had asked the same question yet again.

Houlihan shook his head.

"Let's take the three weeks before the murder: was there anything that made you look twice, or that startled you – anything at all?"

"I'm right, aren't I, that they don't give the death penalty?" said Houlihan.

"In this case, with the decapitation . . . could be an aggravating factor indicating a depraved mind. Don't be too sure about that," said Dure.

"Well, I've got to protect my son. There's years of appeals, anyway, right?"

"Could be . . . or not. Depends how the trial judge conducts the trial. With a confession . . ."

Houlihan averted his gaze from Dure. Dure said, "You wanted to protect your son, so you gave a confession. Did you really think your son had done it?"

"No. But from what the police said, I was worried that they could pin it on him."

"If you didn't do it, and your son didn't do it, then somebody else did. You'll agree with me on that?"

"Yes."

"Whoever that is, is still free and about, and could kill again," said Dure.

Houlihan shrugged.

"Not only do we not know who it was, we don't know the motive. So we can't rule out the possibility that this person has something against your whole family and might even now be keeping watch on your son as his next victim. Isn't that right?" Dure was not being gentle.

Houlihan made a spastic gesture with his hands, and sighed forcefully.

"Maybe," said Dure, "you want to start cooperating with me in earnest, rather than just making a *pro forma* effort. Did you notice anything at all, in the three weeks preceding the murder . . . that startled you, surprised you . . . anything out of the ordinary – anything at all?"

"At the gun show," said Houlihan, "the weekend it happened, Saturday, when business was slow in the afternoon, I closed my trailer for half and hour and went walking around to stretch my legs and get something to eat. Coming the other way was a woman and we looked at each other briefly, like, you know, I think I've seen that person somewhere. She looked away quickly and then veered in a different direction so that we didn't pass each other. I think I may have seen her at the Reform Party Christmas Party last December." He paused. "That's the only thing that I can think of that was out of the ordinary or surprising."

"Do you know her name?"

"No, sir. And maybe I never saw her before. Don't know. It was just strange the way she glanced at me and then changed direction."

"Describe her."

"Maybe five feet, four, brown hair, average build, kinda pretty."

"What was she wearing?"

Houlihan's head swayed from side to side. "A kind of tight-fitting shirt with no buttons – I guess that means it was a pull-over type shirt, shorts, gosh, I don't know the names of women's shoes, some kind of sandals, maybe."

"What else did you notice before the murder that was odd, or out of place? Did you have any visitors to your house?"

"There was the meeting of the Party, but I don't get too much involved with that."

"When was that?"

"The weekend before."

"Was there a guest list?"

"I don't think so. I don't know. I suppose you could look in my wife's papers. She might have one . . . or I think sometimes they have a sign-in sheet."

"Or how about meeting minutes?" asked Dure.

"Yeah, yeah, I think so."

"Who would have those?"

"Don't know."

"Do you know the exact name of the organization?"

"That I don't know either. Something like the Essex County Reform Party Committee or something like that."

"Does your son use steroids?"

Could it have been the sudden change of subject that caused the startled look on Houlihan's face? After a moment he said, sadly, "Not that I know of."

"You've never asked him, point blank?"

"No."

"Your wife had a cell phone, right?"

"She did. She had a Handiphone 700."

"Do you know where it is?"

"I think, I think, it would have been on her. She probably had it in one of her pockets. I haven't seen it."

"When was the last time you called her or she called you using her cell phone?"

"We didn't talk while I was at the gun show – obviously," he added belatedly. "It would have been . . ." – he rolled his eyes up and to his right – "would have been . . . Thursday? I think. I asked her to get some bologna on the way home."

"There wouldn't be any text messages or voicemails on her phone from you that could be incriminating?" asked Dure.

"Not that I am aware of."

"Do you know her password or unlock key?"

Houlihan frowned and shook his head.

"For any of her accounts? Facebook? Bank account?"

Houlihan looked at Dure with anxiety in his eyes. "No."

Dure got from Houlihan his wife's birth date, maiden name, as many favorites as Houlihan could think of, movie, color, etc., name of high school, whatever might possibly serve as a password.

Who knew what might be on the victim's cell phone? It could just as easily be incriminating as exculpatory. Yet faced with the imperative to find the real murderer, Dure had to take risks. He wanted to look into the phone some more.

7.

Dure called Kurt Kniffe and gave him the meager information which Dure had gotten from Houlihan. He wondered, by the bye, whether Kniffe had checked with his police contacts.

"The police are not investigating this case," said Kniffe. "The word is, Preston thinks this case is on ice. They've got a confession and that's enough."

"That's odd," said Dure. "Last I heard, they didn't have the murder weapon, and they didn't have the head. I would think they'd keep looking for those."

"It's been four years since I was on the force, but Lieutenant Gittleson is still there, and if the County Attorney says he's got enough, Gittleson won't go further. Besides, they're busy with the other beheading case."

"What did you find out about that?"

"Let me defer my report until Monday. The weekends are usually very productive for us."

* * *

Monday afternoon at 2:55: Kurt Kniffe finished reviewing a small sheaf of papers, squared them up, and slid them into a manila folder. He put on his suit jacket, took up the folder, and made his way across the building, out of his suite and into Walter Dure's suite. Somehow, when Kniffe trod the old, creaking hallways in that many-times-remodeled building, the floor made no noise. He nodded to Kara, who returned his nod with a smile, which, in the course of their frequent interactions meant, 'go on back.' Kniffe knew the way and walked back to Dure's office. The door was open; Dure was at his desk, apparently lost in concentration in reading a law book. Perhaps out of professional habit, Kniffe paused at the threshold, observing Dure while he considered himself unobserved. The office reminded him of a dingy aquarium, or of a shadowed reef, where a careful observer might notice the tip of a barracuda's snout slightly protruding from a crevice.

"Come in," said Dure, without looking up,

Startled, Kniffe rapped lightly on the door and entered.

Dure wrote a few more words on the legal pad in front of him, put the pad on the open book he had been consulting and closed the book so that the pad became an outsized bookmark. "What do we know about Mrs. Houlihan?" he asked.

Kniffe slid into the chair in front of Dure's desk. He put the manila folder he had brought with him on the floor. "The basic statistics, DOB, SSN, marital status, physical description, address, and so forth I have for you on a summary sheet. As to her co-workers: I have an organizational chart of the County Library Services Department. I also have a list of the people who worked on the same floor with her in the County Services Building.

"The subject was very active politically. She was the immediate past Vice-Chair of the Essex County Reform Party. In one sense, then, everybody in the Greenback Party could have been her enemy. My investigator who talked to people in the County Services Building this morning reports that about a week before she was killed, one Bruno Snodhuis came to her office and had a loud argument with her, apparently about politics. We are in the process of checking this Snodhuis out. Otherwise, on this early-stage investigation, we do not find any specific political enemies." Kniffe paused. His wrists were resting on his thighs, and he lightly pressed the fingertips of one hand against the fingertips of the other. He bowed his head for a moment then looked up.

"As opposed to enemies, however, there is some as yet inconclusive information that she had more-than-friendly relations with a man in her own Reform Party, one Rhys Parker. If you like, we will further develop this information."

"This might lead to the discovery of someone who might wish to harm Mrs. Houlihan?" asked Dure.

Kniffe shrugged. "The betrayed wife, the betrayed husband," he said.

Dure nodded. "Give it another three, four hours."

"The betrayed husband, as in the man who has already made a confession," said Kniffe.

"I get the point," said Dure, in an ironical tone of voice. "What else?"

"Social media: No Facebook account that we can find. She had a Twitter account, mostly political stuff, at least based on what's publicly available. We obviously don't have her sign-in info. She had a smart phone. It's now in the possession of the police.

"We found in the Family Court docket a case Houlihan v. Houlihan. Not much there, but there was a docket entry for a restraining order."

"Can you get the order?" asked Dure.

"The case is more than ten years old, and as you know, the actual documents are not available to the public – just the docket item listing."

"Okay, I'll follow up on that," said Dure. "Since my client presumably was a party, he should be able to get a copy. Anything else? – any information that she used drugs?"

"Nothing on that. Last thing: you asked me to look into the al-Metoosi case further. It appears that he is your standard-issue jihadi. We didn't find any connection between him and our subject."

"Did she post any anti-Muslim sentiments on her Twitter account?" asked Dure.

"None that we saw."

"Thank you for this information," said Dure. "I will follow up on the restraining order and the cell phone. Please find out exactly what was the relationship between Mrs. Houlihan and Mr. Parker."

Kniffe's face was entirely deadpan. He nodded once, stood and silently left the office.

* * *

Dure visited the jail again, Kara with him.

"You are certain that there could be nothing incriminating on your wife's cell phone," he said to Houlihan.

"No, no," replied Houlihan, in a loud voice. "I'm sure I sent nothing. Just what I told you before."

"The bologna?" said Dure.

Houlihan nodded.

"You did not send her a text message or leave a voicemail that implied anger, or violence – or that someone could twist into having such a meaning?"

Houlihan denied it. "You can check my phone. It has all the text messages I sent."

"The prosecution has your cell phone – and your wife's cell phone. If I can get access to them, I assume you can open your own?"

"I should be able to."

"And if I can get access to your wife's phone, could you give me the unlock key, the password, to open it?"

"I don't know about that."

"Do you know any passwords that your wife used?"

Houlihan was slow in answering. "I told you all I know before."

Dure said to Kara, "Give him some paper and a pen," and as she pushed a pad of paper diagonally across the dented metal table top, Dure said to Houlihan, "Do it again. Write down all the possibilities that you can think of that might be passwords your wife used."

While Houlihan wrote and pondered, pondered and wrote, Dure scraped his chair back, stood, and began to pace. With his head bent forward, his chin supported by his left hand, he walked back and forth. His fingers now massaged his chin, now toyed with his lips. At length he returned to his chair and sat down.

"Done?" he said.

Houlihan nodded.

Dure told Kara to give Houlihan three documents which she had prepared back at the office. He instructed Houlihan to sign them. Houlihan glanced at the first document, then signed it. He read the second document, and signed it. After looking at the third document for a moment, he raised his eyes to Dure. "You need this?" he asked.

"I do."

"Okay," said Houlihan, and he scratched his signature on it as well.

* * *

Dure asked prosecutor Roderick Preston to give him Mrs. Houlihan's phone, claiming that it constituted exculpatory evidence which the prosecution was bound to turn over under the Brady rule. Preston was intransigent in his refusal, so Dure filed a motion with the court.

Preston filed a counter-motion, demanding that the defense give the prosecution the unlock code so that the prosecution could open *Mr.* Houlihan's phone.

They argued the motions before Judge Aburnathy, whose manner on the bench was one of cynical nonchalance. The judge was being harangued by Preston:

"The Commonwealth is only required to turn over to the defense exculpatory materials, and only copies at that. Dure has not established that anything on Mrs. Houlihan's phone would be exculpatory, and in any event, there is no way to copy the phone. The Commonwealth certainly is not going to just surrender it to the defense for them to tamper with any way they see fit."

The judge took off his glasses, let them fall on the bench, and rubbed his eyes. Without his glasses, his puffy eyes made him appear hard of seeing, so to speak. He propped his elbows on the bench and intertwined his fingers. He smiled. "Continue, counsel," he said.

"As for Mister Houlihan's phone, I have provided Your Honor with an affidavit of probable cause. The physical phone is in the possession of the prosecution, but without the unlock code, we cannot access the probative evidence which the phone may contain. The Court should order the defense to provide the unlock code for Mr. Houlihan's phone."

"Mr. Dure?" said the judge, turning in Dure's direction, but still not replacing his glasses.

"Your Honor, as to the prosecution's request for Mr. Houlihan's unlock code, the defendant cannot be compelled to testify against himself. That includes any information which might tend to incriminate him. If the prosecution can guess the code or run some program to discover it, that's the prosecution's business. But the prosecution cannot compel my client to testify."

"As for Mrs. Houlihan's phone, justice requires the state, with all its superior investigative resources, to make available to the defense any information which may tend to exculpate the defendant. In theory at least, and it's a theory to which the Supreme Court has subscribed in the Brady case, the prosecution's job is to pursue justice, not simply win cases."

Mr. Preston interrupted. "The defense has not established that there is anything exculpatory on Mrs. Houlihan's phone. In fact, nobody knows what may be on that phone. The prosecution is not obliged to hand over evidence on the basis of mere speculation that it might be exculpatory."

"It seems to me," said the judge, putting on his glasses, "that a so-called smart phone, such as is at issue here, is like a document. It is well established that a defendant must surrender documents in response to a search warrant, and that doing so does not violate his right not to testify, with the caveat, that the defendant cannot be compelled to authenticate the documents. There is nothing incriminating in an unlock code *per se*, and so it seems to me that I could order the defendant to provide it to the prosecution, providing that it is done through counsel and that such provision not be used by the prosecution as authentication. However," said the judge, turning to Preston, "I believe you have a confession in this case?"

"We do Your Honor."

"Then," said the judge, "the phone is not a critical piece of evidence, especially since your affidavit of probable cause is rather weak."

"I might point out to the Court," said Preston, "that the existence of a signed, written confession seems to be of no moment to Mr. Dure, who is defending with vigor, notwithstanding the defendant's confession."

The judge nodded. Turning to Dure, he said, "Your claim of exculpatory evidence with regard to Mrs. Houlihan's phone is, if anything, even weaker than the prosecution's affidavit of probable cause. What I think I'm going to do is deny both motions and leave the parties where they are – rather than get into what might be complex wrangling about possession and copying and monitoring what the other party is doing with these electronic devices. But it has been a pleasure to have you in my courtroom. Is the case proceeding on track for our trial date?"

Both counsel assented.

"And plea negotiations are ongoing as well?" asked the judge.

Dure looked at Preston, and Preston looked at Dure. There was some hesitation. Dure said, "As appropriate for this case. I have always found Mr. Preston to be amenable to discussions."

"Thank you, counsel," said the judge. "Next is Commonwealth vs. Plympton."

* * *

The meeting which took place six days later had something of the air of a prisoner exchange. Prosecutor Preston and his associate, Jessica Tinder, Lieutenant Wisdom of the Canterbury police force, and a computer technician, all sat on one side of a large conference table in an ultra-modern conference room in the Justice Complex of Essex County. On the other side sat Dure, Ralph Hartley, Kara, and a free-lance computer technician whom Dure had retained through the good offices of Kurt Kniffe and Associates.

After their fruitless adventures in court, Dure and Preston had negotiated a deal: the prosecution would make Mrs. Houlihan's phone available, and the defense would provide the unlock code. Both sides would then get to see whatever was on it.

It was a risky deal for Dure. If there was some incriminating evidence on the phone, he would be making a gift to the prosecution – a gift which might in fact kill his client. That is why one of the papers he had had Houlihan sign was a written assurance by Houlihan that there would be no incriminating evidence, and an instruction to Dure to pursue this evidence. The justification for running the risk was that with a confession in the case, Dure had to find out who, other than his client, had murdered Mrs. Houlihan. Assuming that his client was telling the truth, the recent communications by Mrs. Houlihan before she had been murdered might provide a lead to the murderer.

The prosecutor, Roderick Preston, was a tall, patrician-appearing man. The extra ten pounds which he carried on his frame were well distributed and not excessive for a man in his fifties. Tortoise-shell glasses rested on his large nose, and his neat, combed hair was probably dyed. On the table in front of him was the three inch by six inch phone of Mrs. Houlihan.

Attorneys like to argue. Notwithstanding that they had agreed on this exchange, the two attorneys chewed up half an hour arguing; it became uncertain whether the exchange would actually take place.

After a curt exchange of pleasantries, Preston said, "Why don't you write down the unlock key and give it to our computer tech, Shawn here, and he'll unlock the phone."

Dure replied, "What we have is a list of possible unlock codes from my client. They are naturally attorney-client privileged, and obviously, at most only one of them will work. So I can't disclose all of them to you. I think a better way of proceeding will be for you to give the phone to my tech guy here, and he will try them out until one of them works."

"Are you telling me you don't have the unlock code?" said Preston. "What's your game here?"

"Do you know the code to unlock your wife's phone?" asked Dure.

"That's neither here nor there," said Preston.

"Exactly," said Dure. "Mr. Houlihan has some educated guesses as to his wife's unlock code, but he might be wrong. There's nothing wrong with us trying them out."

"I should point out," interposed the prosecution's computer expert, "that the way the operating system on that phone works is that repeated attempts to unlock the phone with incorrect codes lengthens the delay for you to enter another code. Otherwise, we would have cracked the code ourselves by now. After the fourth incorrect attempt, you have to wait a minute before you can try again. After the next incorrect guess, you have to wait five minutes. After the next one, ten minutes. After ten incorrect guesses, you have to wait an hour between each attempt. So, if you've got a lot of candidates to try out, we might be here a long time."

"You're not going to waste my time with a trick like this," said Preston. He palmed the phone with his large hand and put it in his pocket.

"I didn't come here to waste your time or mine," said Dure.

"I should also point out," the prosecution's computer expert spoke up again, "that we've tried a number of common unlock codes, so that the quota of ten quick attempts has been used up. Right now, we're at one hour between tries."

On Dure's side of the table, everyone but Dure himself blanched at this information.

"You led me to believe that you had *the* unlock code," said Preston, using his best jury-argument mode of indignant accusation.

"I think we do have *the* unlock code," returned Dure, "it's just that we also have some others. It's going to be a simple matter of deciding which of our candidates is the most likely to be the right one. We'll agree, to be considerate of the other demands on your time, to make only one attempt. If that doesn't work, we're done."

Again, on Dure's side of the table, everyone but Dure himself blanched at this offer.

"I'll agree to that," said Preston, "if you'll give me your list of candidates if the one you pick doesn't work."

"No," said Dure. "Your tech here obviously will try them out at leisure, and when one of them works, you'll have the contents of the phone and we'll have nothing. Besides, as I said before, these communications are attorney-client privileged."

"How can a supposed unlock code be attorney-client privileged?" demanded Preston.

"Just to speak hypothetically," said Dure, "possible unlock codes might be a significant date, or place name, or some other piece of information that you might use for investigation – not to mention that if I gave you this information you might claim waiver of the attorney-client privilege and seek more attorney-client communications."

"That's ridiculous," sniffed Preston.

"It may be ridiculous, but I noticed you didn't say you wouldn't do it," said Dure.

The temperature in the room was starting to rise.

"Look," said Dure, in a calmer tone of voice, "you want to know what's on the phone, otherwise, you wouldn't have had your technician try to open it. We've got eight people assembled here. The phone is here. Possible unlock codes are here. It won't take but thirty seconds for us to try one, and if it doesn't work, we're out of here. Why waste eight people's time?"

Preston reached in his pocket and brought the phone back out.

Dure took from one of his pockets a slip of paper. He turned to Ralph on his left and motioned the computer tech to huddle with them. In very low tones they debated which of the codes to try. After a few moments, Dure pointed to a particular entry on the paper and asked the technician, "Got it?"

"Yeah, got it."

Dure refolded the paper and put it back in his pocket. The huddle broke up.

"Okay, we're ready," said Dure.

Preston nodded to his technician who got up and went around the table to stand behind Dure's technician. Preston gave the phone a shove, and it slid across the table to the technician. Dure also got up and stood behind the technician. Dure was looking over the tech's right shoulder, and the prosecution's technician was looking over his left.

Josh, Dure's technician, took up the phone and pressed the start button. A virtual keypad appeared on the phone's screen.

Preston now also got up and came around the table. He was tall enough that he could look over his own technician's shoulder to see what Dure's technician was doing.

The technician had already pressed three numbers. He had three more numbers to go. The room was quiet and all eyes were watching him.

He pressed a three. He pressed an eight.

"No! It was a seven," said Ralph. "The fifth number was a seven."

The technician stopped. "It was an eight," he said. He looked to Dure for confirmation.

"I think it was an eight," said Dure. He pulled out his slip of paper. "It was an eight," he said.

The technician punched in the last number, a seven.

The screen went blank momentarily. Then, the virtual keypad re-appeared on the phone's screen. The code had failed. Groans of disappointment sounded. "Let me see that," said Dure, and before Preston could object, he reached down and took the phone out of his technician's hands. He carefully placed his right thumb on the start button and rested it there. The screen went blank again. In a moment, colorful icons appeared, as if floating to the surface of a pond. "It works!" he said.

"What!"

"How the hell . . ."

"What are you doing?" said Preston, suspiciously.

Dure pressed the icon to bring up recent calls. Then he put the phone on the table so that everyone could see. "Last phone call," he read out loud, "Nine thirty-two p. m. . . . June 5! That's the day she was killed. This changes everything!"

Josh was opening his laptop computer and attaching a cable.

"My tech will take a copy of the phone, then you can have it," said Dure.

"What's the unlock code?" demanded Preston.

"I don't know," said Dure. "But why do you need it? The phone is unlocked."

"Yes, but it will lock up again," said Preston. "We need that code."

"I don't have the code. You saw that the one we tried didn't work."

"It did work. The phone's open. This is another of your underhanded tricks. I'm not going to put up with it."

"In the first place," replied Dure, "you can keep it from locking up again. Just have someone swipe the screen every two minutes." He laughed.

Preston growled.

"In second place," said Dure, "your tech can make a copy just like mine is doing."

"I want that code," said Preston in a cold, menacing voice.

"Alright," said Dure. "If you'll give me your word that you will not treat my giving you the code as a waiver of the attorney-client privilege, I'll give you the code that my tech just used."

"Okay," said Preston, after some hesitation.

"Josh, write down for Mr. Preston the code you just used – but remember," said Dure, turning to Preston, "it doesn't work. You just saw it."

"I'm not sure what I saw, other than some of your trickery," said Preston.

* * *

In the elevator on the way down, Dure's computer technician asked him, with a wonder of admiration in his eyes, "How did you do that?"

Dure made a subtle gesture with his eyes and pointed a forefinger held at waist level towards a woman in the elevator who was not of their party. The technician got the message and said nothing more.

Once they were outside the Justice Center, and walking towards Dure's office across the street, Dure said, "We have urgent work to do. We've got to get all the leads off that phone and follow them up before the prosecution gets to those witnesses. We'll set up a war room in the office, I'll call Kurt Kniffe off whatever else he is working on. That last phone call that we looked at, that must have been to someone in her contacts list. It said 'R. Parker.'"

"Right," said the technician.

"That's got to be the same Rhys Parker that Kniffe mentioned to me."

By this time they had arrived at the door to Dure's office.

8.

Once inside, Dure held an impromptu meeting with the four of them standing right there in the reception area. "The first order of business is to talk to this Rhys Parker. If he can say that he talked with Mrs. Houlihan at 9:32, that will go a long way towards exonerating our client."

"This could win the case for us," said Kara excitedly.

"Not by itself," said Dure. "It's going to be really hard to overcome a confession. But if this information pans out, the prosecution will have to argue something like Houlihan driving back in the middle of the night, and then returning to the gun show. The more we can make the prosecution have to twist its arguments into a pretzel, the better. And, we could search for evidence that would show that Houlihan didn't drive back. This could be a a major development in the case."

"I always thought the son did it," said Ralph.

"But we have to hurry," said Dure. "If the prosecution gets to Parker first, they may scare him off from talking to us, and they will probably seize his phone. Preston is probably having a search warrant drafted as we speak. Good thing is, that may delay them by twenty minutes or so, so we have a little head start."

Dure handed out instructions. "Kara, you find out the office and home address of this Rhys Parker, and as many phone numbers as you can. See if you can find out where he is right now. Don't disclose where you are calling from – we don't want to scare him off.

To the computer tech he said, "Josh, get me all the details about that last call on Mrs. Houlihan's phone: start time, end time, see if you can get the actual number that was called, whatever there is. Get that to me right away. Then, make a list of all the calls, incoming and outgoing, and all the text messages in the twenty-four hours before . . . let's make it back to Thursday noon.

"Ralph, you're going to come with me to visit Mr. Parker – just as soon as Kara tells us where he is."

The little group broke up and each went to his work space.

* * *

In Prosecutor Preston's office in the Justice Center, the relatively inexperienced Jessica Tinder was being given direction by Preston. "Dure said that a conversation by the victim at nine thirty would change everything. I think he's grasping at straws. I've never lost a case with a confession in it. I'm not going to lose this one either. Nobody confesses to murder unless they're guilty, especially not someone who lives in a neighborhood like Sunderly Chase. This guy is not some scared fifteen-year old. I want you to go over Houlihan's confession and see if anything in there is inconsistent with a nine thirty conversation. Have Shawn make a list of all the contacts in that phone for the week preceding the murder and get that list to Lt. Wisdom."

Ms. Tinder was scribbling notes in her rounded handwriting on a yellow legal pad which she supported, while sitting with her legs crossed, on her left thigh. "Okay, got it," she said. She stood and left Preston's office with an earnest demeanor. She had never been on a murder case before.

In her own small office, she pulled up a copy of the transcription of Houlihan's videotaped confession on her computer screen:

> My name is Howard Houlihan. I am making this statement of my free will. I have been advised of my right to remain silent and my right to legal counsel, and I hereby waive my rights.
>
> I live at nine Cherry Lane in Sunderly Chase. On Friday, June 5, I left my home to drive to Belleterre to go to a gun show for the purpose of selling Hawaiian shave ice. As I was leaving . . . uh, going out the door, around one o'clock, [by Detective Johnson: that's one in the afternoon?] right . . . my wife and I got into an argument. She became very violent and abusive. Somehow, I hit her in the head with my fist and she fell down. I did not mean to kill her, but she became dead. I panicked and to cover up what had happened, I cut off her head and put the body outside the house to make it look like a Muslim had killed her.
>
> After this, my memory is a blank and I cannot remember what I did with the head, nor with the knife I used to cut it off. The next thing I do remember is setting up my vending trailer in the parking lot at the gun show in Belleterre on Friday afternoon, about four o'clock.
>
> When I returned home Monday morning, I was at first surprised to find that my wife was dead. I called the police. When the police came, I showed them the

body. They questioned me. At that time, I
was nervous and didn't want to say
anything, and said nothing to the police
about what I had done.

Now I want to admit what I did so that
the community will no longer worry and so
that innocent people will not come under
suspicion.

I make this statement freely, without
any compulsion.

Signed: Howard Houlihan

On first reading through this statement, Jessica
Tinder thought there was a problem. So she read
through it again, slowly. Jeez, Louise, there's a problem
here – a big problem. And she was the one who
discovered it – if she was right. But it was so simple, she
couldn't be wrong. Her named flashed in bright lights,
her star was rising, and her breathing quickened. She
printed out a copy of the statement and practically ran
to prosecutor Preston's office.

His door was open. She slowed to a brisk walk and
entered. He was sitting sideways, intent on his
computer screen, upright in his starched white shirt
and blue-and-red rep tie. Perhaps the noise of her entry
or a glimpse of her in his peripheral vision caught his
attention; he turned his head, but not his torso, in her
direction. "Yes?" he said.

"The confession says early afternoon. If she was
alive at nine thirty, we've got a problem," she
announced.

"Let me see."

She handed the paper to him. He glanced over it
quickly, then pressed a button to activate his speaker

phone. He tapped three numbers on the phone. A voice came out of the phone, "Shawn here."

"Shawn, get me all the details on the last calls made on Mrs. Houlihan's phone."

"Got 'em already."

"Are they in a form that you can e-mail them?"

"Absolutely."

"Send them *now* to Lt. Wisdom."

"Okay," said Shawn.

Preston clicked off the call. To Jessica he said, "Thank you. We'll look into this. Things are not always what they seem." While she was leaving his office, Preston was looking up Lt. Wisdom's telephone number.

* * *

Kara walked into Dure's office. She had in her hand a pink While-You-Were-Out slip on which she had written an address. She said, "Mr. Parker runs a real estate brokerage. He is spending this afternoon at the model home in a new development called Chestnut Hills. Here's the address," handing the pink slip to Dure. "I figured the streets might not be in the GPS database yet, so I also wrote down the intersection where the development's entrance is."

"Smart girl," said Dure. "Thanks." He was putting on his suit jacket. "Call Kurt Kniffe and tell him to meet me there. I've already given him a heads up." To Ralph he said, "Come on." They hurried out of the office.

Ralph drove Dure's car. "I know where it is," said Ralph. "Out Route 322. There's lots of signs." Chestnut Hills was six miles out of town. As soon as they were clear of town traffic and stop lights, Ralph bumped the speed to seventy, and they flew.

"Ralph, I don't want to get stopped for speeding for the sake of saving sixty seconds," said Dure.

"I don't see no cops," said Ralph.

"Slow down," said Dure.

Ralph took his foot off the gas. The road was straight and level. They could see far ahead, and in the mirrors, far behind. There were no cars in sight going in their direction. So either the police and Kniffe were far ahead of them, or far behind.

Ralph had been right. There were lots of signs. "New Homes starting in the low $400's," said signs flanked by attention-getting pennants, flapping in the breeze.

If the people who write laundry detergent advertisements for the television could dictate their idea of suburban perfection, it would be the model home and sales office for the Chestnut Hills development. It had a smooth, macadam driveway, a neat lawn, a concrete walkway with a cute, superfluous curve leading to a front stoop over which was a gabled portico. The front door was oak veneer with an elaborate, translucent window and matching side panels. Immediately inside was a large, high-ceilinged foyer and a sales agent sitting at a small desk.

Standing in front of the sales agent's desk, apparently talking with him, was a man of middle height, a nondescript man in a gray suit. When Dure and Ralph entered the foyer, Mr. nondescript turned and greeted Dure. "Hello, Walter," he said.

"Hello, Kurt," said Dure.

"This is Rhys Parker," said Kniffe. Turning to the sales agent, he said, "Mr. Parker, this is Walter Dure, the attorney I had mentioned to you."

"I've told Mr. Parker the basic situation," said Kniffe to Dure. "He has surprising information."

Rhys Parker rose from his chair and shook hands with Dure. Ralph stood in the background, watching.

Parker seemed to think there might be the prospect of a sale somewhere in this situation with two men apparently of substance and some kind of hanger-on, notwithstanding what Kniffe had told him and notwithstanding that no wives were present. Moreover, he was very uncomfortable talking about Tiffany Houlihan. Therefore, using a presumptive lead, he took a couple of steps towards the kitchen while saying, "Can I show you around the house?"

Dure said, "I don't want to waste your time. Mr. Kniffe has told you, I take it, that we're interested in a telephone call Tiffany Houlihan made to you on the evening of June 5, shortly before she was killed."

Parker smiled nervously. He was perspiring. "As I said, as I said to Mr. Kniffe, I didn't talk with her that evening. We can talk as we walk. The houses in this development are custom built," he was speaking rapidly and continuing to walk towards the kitchen, "and are upscale in design and materials. Even if," (he wanted to forestall the objection which in the circumstances was obvious) "you are not in the market, you may have clients who would be interested in a house here –" He turned his back now to them all and walked to the kitchen, forcing them to follow.

The kitchen was spacious and flooded with light from the afternoon sun. Dure said, "Mr. Parker, we have seen Mrs. Houlihan's phone, and it shows that a call of about six minutes duration was made to you at nine thirty that evening."

Parker retreated to the other side of the island in the kitchen and faced Dure and company across it. "I didn't talk to her. It must be a mistake."

"If it's a mistake," said Dure, "we needn't keep you long. Your number is 289-3760?"

Parker nodded.

"That's the number that was on Mrs. Houlihan's phone. Let's do this. Show us your phone's log of calls received. If the call's not there . . . we're done."

"How do I know?" said Parker. "She might have called me, I have no control over that, but I didn't talk to her. Even if there's a call to my phone, that doesn't mean that I talked to her."

"True," admitted Dure.

An awkward moment ensued in which no one said anything.

"You don't have to talk to us," said Dure. "But that makes you suspicious. And this is a murder case. Inquiries may get insistent. Various forms of legal process could come into play."

Parker looked uncomfortable. His face glistened and his body showed a sort of jumpiness, as if he wanted to run away, but was forcing himself to stand where he was.

Kniffe took from his right trousers pocket a thin fold of bills and held it below the island, out of Parker's sight. They were fifties and hundreds which he carried with him to act as a catalyst to assistance, on occasions when he thought it would be helpful. He separated out a hundred dollar bill. "You have, as it seems, nothing to hide; and if nothing to hide, nothing to fear. I realize that we are taking your time, for which we are willing to compensate you." He palmed the folded hundred dollar bill, and sliding his hand onto the center of the island, lifted his hand, exposing the hundred. He withdrew his hand, leaving the bill.

"You keep your phone in your hands," said Dure, using a presumptive approach himself, and walking around the island to approach Parker. "We don't need to touch it. Just let us review the log of incoming calls. You bring it up, we'll just watch. And," he added, "when we're done, I'll let you know a bit of useful information."

"Okay, because," said Parker, feeling himself in a tight spot, "I really did not talk to her, and it appears that this is the only way to convince you." He took out his phone and placed it on the island countertop.

Kniffe and Dure came around the island from opposite directions. Dure stood to Parker's left, and Kniffe to his right. Ralph came up to the island and occupied the place where Dure and Kniffe had been standing.

Parker tapped his phone several times. "Okay," he said, "here's the missed calls list."

"Scroll down to June 5," said Dure.

Parker swiped the phone a couple of times with his thumb. Then he touched the phone to stop the scrolling and with his forefinger moved the image a bit and steadied it.

"There it is," said Dure. "So she did call."

"Right," said Parker, "but this is the 'missed calls' log. I didn't talk to her."

"There's a voicemail message," said Dure. "Let's hear it. It could be very important. Even a matter of life and death."

Parker looked at him.

"It has nothing to do with you," said Dure. "If she was alive at that time, it could prove that my client didn't kill her."

The air was fraught with tension, and perhaps Parker was curious himself, or perhaps he knew what was on the voicemail, having listened to it himself before. In any event, Parker tapped the voicemail icon, tapped again to turn on the speaker feature, and took his hand from the phone.

A sort of dull hissing began to play. It continued, modulating slightly in tone. This continued for over five minutes, and then stopped.

"Pocket dial," said Parker. "Must have been."

When Dure experienced emotion, there were almost no external signs of it. The only one was that his breathing came noisily through his nostrils. This happened now. His facial expression did not change. "Where were you when this call came in?" he said.

"I've given you what you wanted," said Parker, now seeming to feel that he had the upper hand. "That's all you're getting."

"Alright," said Dure. "I thank you. But don't you want to know who killed Mrs. Houlihan?"

Parker shrugged his shoulders. "What's she to me?" he said. "I've got a business to run."

Kniffe said, from Parker's other side, in a sort of ambush, "But you did work with her in Reform Party matters? I have it on good authority."

"Gentlemen," said Parker, turning to Kniffe – Parker's smile was bright and toothy but his eyes were narrowed – "if you know of anyone in the market for a new home, this development is *the* prestige development in the Canterbury area." He took from his pocket a small block of business cards, and dealt one to each of the three men.

Dure and Kniffe and Ralph began to walk out of the kitchen, in the direction from which they had come. Parker stayed behind the island, and the hundred dollar bill remained on the island, untouched. At the doorway, Dure stopped and turned. "I promised you a piece of information," he said. "It's this: I would not be surprised if the police came for your phone with a subpoena."

In the driveway Dure and company stood for a few moments, talking.

Dure, the man of frowning mien, said, "Kurt, find out as much as you can about Mr. Parker. I really want to know what was the relationship between him and the decedent. And, where was he and what was he doing at the time of the murder?"

"What are we calling the time of the murder?" asked Kniffe. "Is it still from Friday morning to Saturday afternoon?"

"I guess it'll have to be," said Dure. "This evidence didn't narrow it down, as I had hoped it would – what do you think?" he asked. "Even to make a pocket dial, she would have had to be alive at the time?"

Kniffe was noncommittal. "It's possible. Or, the phone could have been in somebody else's possession – the murderer's perhaps?"

"My understanding," said Dure, "is that the police recovered the phone from the body. Maybe that's worth double-checking."

"Maybe," said Ralph, "she started to make the call and was interrupted by the murderer."

"But there was nothing on the voicemail recording other than basically silence," said Dure. "If she had been interrupted, we should have heard voices, or the phone being dropped, or something. Maybe we should listen to the voicemail again." He took out his phone and made a call.

"Kara? . . . I want you to make up a subpoena right now for the Houlihan trial for . . ." Dure paused for a moment to phrase his thoughts, "all messages, voicemail recordings, communications in written or electronic form by, between, to, and/or from Tiffany Houlihan and Rhys Parker during the time period from May 1 through June 8.' . . . put my electronic signature on it, and text me an electronic copy right now, as soon as you can. . . . Okay, right, thanks."

To Kniffe he said, "We've got Parker's phone number, right."

"Of course."

"As soon as I get the subpoena, I'll text it to him. Then we'll go in and talk to him again. Let's go sit in my car."

"Maybe he's erasing the message right now," said Ralph.

Dure huffed a loud sigh, turned on his heel, and went back to the model home. Kniffe and Ralph followed.

Inside, Parker was again at the sales desk. His phone was out on the desk top and he was tapping it. As Dure entered the foyer, Parker looked up sharply, guiltily.

Dure said, "I realized I shouldn't assume things, and although it was clear to me, maybe it was not clear to you that you should not erase that voicemail message – nor any other messages you might have gotten from Mrs. Houlihan."

"Why, and who said so?"

"It's evidence in a criminal investigation and the law says so."

Parker shrugged his shoulders.

"You haven't erased it, have you?" asked Dure.

"No," said Parker sullenly.

A ding sounded from Dure's phone. He began to tap its screen.

Kniffe moved forward and engaged Parker. "You live in the same development as Mrs. Houlihan," he said.

Ralph wandered off into other parts of the model home.

Dure tapped "Send," and a moment later a ding sounded from Parker's phone.

The front door opened.

"I've just served you with a subpoena," said Dure to Parker, "for that voicemail message –"

Lt. Wisdom came in through the front door.

"-- and any other similar messages from Mrs. Houlihan."

"And I have a subpoena for the phone itself," said Lt. Wisdom. He was a small man and slender, almost slight, except that he had thick, muscular forearms. His short hair was all white. He advanced to the desk at which Parker was sitting. "Are you Rhys Parker?"

"Yes."

He took a folded paper from a pocket, opened it up, and waved it at Parker. "I have a search warrant. Is that your phone? Give it to me."

"I need this phone. It's got all my calendar and contacts. You can't take it."

"You've got it backed up?" said Wisdom.

With a shrugging, surrendering kind of head bob, Parker admitted that he had. Wisdom held out his hand.

"If I might suggest," said Dure to Parker. "You ought to read the warrant and see if it's valid and if what it asks for actually includes your phone."

"This man your client?" demanded Wisdom.

"No," said Dure.

"Then I would advise you, counselor, not to interfere with a police investigation. It's a criminal offense, you know."

Parker held out his hand for the paper which Lt. Wisdom had shown. The lieutenant gave to him, and he began to read it.

Wisdom turned to Dure. "You should be working on negotiating a plea deal, rather than causing trouble.

Your guy is going down, and you know it. You put up a hard fight on a losing case and you don't make any friends in the County Attorney's Office."

"Or with the police, I take it," said Dure.

"You got that right. I've got other work to do besides chasing down nonsense on a case where the investigation is done – and an open-and-shut case if I ever saw one."

'You've found the murder weapon then?" said Dure.

Wisdom glared at him. "We've got your guy's confession. It's all we need."

"Where's the head?" said Dure.

"It's on the port side, amidships – ha, ha," said Wisdom.

"I see you're at sea," said Dure.

Lt. Wisdom turned to Parker. "Done with your legal analysis?" he asked, and he reached down and took the phone. "I'll take the warrant too, if you're done with it."

Parker dropped the paper on the desk.

Wisdom took it up. Turning to Kniffe, whom he had up until then ignored, he asked, "How does it feel, Kurt, working for the dark side?"

Kniffe narrowed his eyes to slits and smiled. "How are you, Harold?"

Lt. Wisdom huffed through his nose in disdainful acknowledgment of the greeting. "I always thought better of you, Kurt. You were one of our best."

"We're all seekers after truth," said Kniffe.

"To protect the public and see that justice is done," said Lt. Wisdom. "That's our mission." Looking at Dure he said, "Too bad the legal system is more interested in technicalities." He paused. "I don't like lawyers," he said. And letting that remark serve as his good-bye, he left.

9.

Courtrooms in the Justice Complex were on the third floor. A long corridor stretched some three hundred feet from the bank of elevators to the other end of the building. Along this corridor were five courtrooms on each side. Up-to-date LED lights threw bright circles of light on the corridor floor, but there were not enough of them to make the whole corridor bright, and the margins of the corridor remained in twilit obscurity with undulating accumulations of dimness swelling to peaks at the midpoints between the bright spots. No artwork adorned the cinder block walls, which had been painted institutional pastel blue.

The hearing on Dure's Motion to Suppress Confession was scheduled for 10:00 a.m. in courtroom 308, the fourth courtroom down, on the left side. Dure had arrived at 9:35 carrying his briefcase, in which were his motion papers and examination notes. Kara had brought a large document case on rollers, containing exhibits, some files, and the laptop computer. At 9:40, two sheriff's deputies brought in Houlihan, handcuffed.

"Please take off the cuffs," said Dure.

The deputies complied.

Houlihan sat at the defense table, next to Dure. He hunched up his shoulders and rubbed his wrists. The two deputies sat in chairs behind Houlihan.

"Wish yourself luck," said Dure to Houlihan. To Houlihan's blank expression, Dure whispered, "We've gone over this. This motion is the whole ball game. If we can get the confession suppressed, you have a reasonable chance for an acquittal. If not . . .."

Houlihan gave him a weak smile.

In the meantime, Preston and his team had come into the courtroom and occupied the prosecution's table.

One spectator had appeared: a man appearing to be in his fifties. His body was wide; he was bald and had a large, full beard, mostly white with some rust color to it. He resembled Santa Claus.

Dure got up and introduced himself. "I'm Walter Dure."

"I know. My name is Torvald Bornstein." His teeth were stained and gaps were between them. "I run the 'Coke's Law Blog'?" he paused upon this questioning note, seeking an acknowledgment from Dure that he was familiar with his website.

Dure smiled and nodded.

"Of course I know who Walter Dure is," continued Bornstein. "For my readers, could you give me any insight into today's hearing?"

"I can't say anything extensive, because as you see, the hearing is about to start. We think we have a good case to make that the confession taken from my client was coerced, not voluntary, and should be suppressed."

"I've been following the case," said Bornstein. "It's an interesting case."

"Let me know if you get any tips as to who the perpetrator might be," said Dure, smiling sardonically.

Bornstein laughed heartily. "Sure thing. Good luck to you." As Dure sidled out of the narrow space between the long, long spectator benches, Bornstein began tapping quietly on the keys of his tablet computer.

On returning from the spectator seating to the well of the court, Dure went over to Preston and shook hands. They had been adversaries a number of times over the years. Preston was at his best before a judge.

Although juries often were resistant to his charm, judges seemed to either like, or be intimidated by, his tall, patrician presence.

Dure returned to the defense table. To Houlihan's gaze of mute inquiry he said, "Even when there's no jury, it's important to understand, and if possible control, the atmosphere of the courtroom. Therefore, I wanted to know who is sitting in the courtroom and what his interest is. That fellow is a legal blogger. I don't think he'll be a problem for us."

The clock on the wall showed three minutes before ten o'clock. The bustle of arranging papers and briefcases, books and bags, and the murmur of nervous conversation had died down, and a silent tension began to throttle the courtroom. The attorneys sat immobile.

The second hand on the clock in the courtroom had spun off another thirty seconds, and the sound of someone clearing his throat resounded, then hung in the air, as if the sustaining pedal on a piano were depressed. In another moment silence had swallowed up the echo.

Dure sat with his left leg crossed over his right. The crease on his trousers was sharp; his black leather wingtips gleamed; and his slender foot neither bounced nor trembled.

A small buzz sounded, "ALL RISE!" shouted the bailiff. With a rushing sound like a gust of wind, everyone in the courtroom stood. The judge came in through a door to the left of and behind the bench, ascended the steps to the bench without hurry, and sat in the large judge's chair. "Take your seats," he said in a conversational tone of voice. He sighed, then opened a folder on the bench in front of him. "This is Commonwealth v. Houlihan, the defense's Motion to

Suppress Confession." he said. "Are counsel ready to proceed?"

"Ready, Your Honor," said two voices, almost simultaneously.

"I will allow counsel three minutes each for an opening statement. Mr. Dure?"

"May it please the Court," began Dure, "the evidence which we will adduce at this hearing will show – and there will be no dispute about these facts – that at the time the statement of confession was signed, the defendant, Mr. Houlihan, was represented by counsel and that he had asserted his Miranda rights. He had told the police that he did not wish to speak to them, and at that time the police did in fact honor the request. Further, the evidence will show that later the police held Mr. Houlihan unreasonably long in custody, misrepresented to him the facts of their investigation, made both threats and promises to such an extent that, under all of these circumstances, Mr. Houlihan's will was overborne; so that the confession must be treated as coerced and involuntary, and therefore must be suppressed as a violation of the defendant's Fifth Amendment rights."

"Thank you counselor," said the judge. "Mr. Preston?"

"Your honor, this is a desperate motion, a hail-Mary pass, as it were, by Mr. Dure, who realizes that he has a hopeless case. The evidence will show that the conversation which resulted in the defendant's full and free confession of the murder of his wife, whom he had grown to hate, was initiated by the defendant – at a time when he was not in custody; that the defendant voluntarily accompanied a police officer to the station where he voluntarily continued the discussion he had started. Furthermore – and this is important – even though the defendant had been given Miranda warnings before, he was given renewed Miranda warnings on this occasion. He waived these warnings and truthfully confessed his crime. Your Honor will see this confession on a videotaped recording.

"To say that a fifty-one year-old man had his will overborne by totally non-violent police questioning is a grasping at straws by a defense which has no defense."

Torvald Bornstein began tapping softly on the keypad of his tablet computer.

"Mr. Dure," said the judge, "call your first witness."

"I call Howard Houlihan."

Reporting on the defense's motion to suppress the confession in the Houlihan case. [post] (Bornstein posted this entry to his live blog. He had to be quiet and surreptitious, because if the judge found out that he was live-blogging from the courtroom, he could get a painful whack – the worst case would be to be found in contempt of court and jailed.) *It doesn't look good for the defense. Prosecutor Preston seems to be in good form and made a forceful opening statement.* [post]

Houlihan was sworn and took the stand. Dure asked him to simply relate what had happened.

"I was on my way home when my truck ran off the road. I don't actually remember going off the road, but I remember waking up, or coming to, as some medics opened the door of my truck."

"And then what happened?"

Attorney Dure is putting his client on the stand. This could be considered a waiver of his client's privilege against self-incrimination, but probably the confession itself was a waiver. However, if Dure can get the confession suppressed, that instance of waiver would be out of the case. So by putting his client on the stand, Dure is risking a waiver which otherwise would not occur. I'd say he's loading his whole case onto this motion. If he wins, his client has a chance; if he loses, not only will the confession come into evidence, but the prosecution will be able to call his client to the stand and question him about whatever testimony he gives at this hearing. [post]

"I was a little dazed, but I wasn't hurt, so I didn't want to go to the hospital." Houlihan was slumped forward slightly in the witness chair, with his forearms resting on his thighs. He therefore had to make an effort to hold his head upright to look Dure in the eye, and this gave him an appearance of coerced alertness. He continued:

"A policeman was there. He asked me what happened. I told him I wasn't really sure, and he called a tow truck. So while we were waiting for the tow truck, we were just chatting, and he said, 'You're the Houlihan whose wife was murdered?' and I said, yes, and he said he was sorry. And the tow truck came and I was going to ride with my truck to Mike's Garage, but the officer asked me did I have a ride home from there, and I said, no, and he said he would give me a ride home.

"So, I let the tow truck take my truck to Mike's and I got in the police car with the officer."

"Did you get into the front seat or the back seat?" asked Dure.

"The front seat. He was going to take me home, it wasn't an arrest or anything," said Houlihan.

"Go on," said Dure.

"The officer said how sorry he was for me, and it must be a hard blow to lose your wife that way, and then he said, 'You know, we're working hard to solve this case,' and he took a turn which was the wrong way to go to my home and he said, 'You know, you could help us clear up a couple of questions, help us solve this case,' and he said 'Would you mind coming to the station for a few minutes.'

"And what did you say?" asked Dure.

"I said, 'If I can help, sure.'"

"Go on," said Dure.

"So, he took me to the station and they put me in a room, and said they'd be right with me, it was just a couple of questions that I could help them with, but then nobody came back and it must have been at least an hour."

"Sorry to interrupt," said Dure. "But up until this point did you at any time initiate a discussion about the murder of your wife?"

"No, no. It was the officer who brought it up."

"Continue," said Dure.

"Then finally a man came in and he was one of the detectives that I had seen on the day that my wife was . . . killed. And he was harsh and unfriendly and he says, 'We know you did it, Houlihan. Why don't you stop lying and tell the truth. It'll go easier on you if you do.'"

"And what did you say?"

"I didn't say anything. He didn't give me a chance. He just continued in a very threatening manner, 'What I'm going to do, Houlihan, is read you your rights.' And in a loud and threatening voice he read from a card he held, 'You have the right to remain silent,' and so on."

"Alright, and then what happened? – Just a minute. About what time was this?"

"It was late in the morning when my truck got in that accident. It must have been about noon or a little later that we got to the police station, so this must have been between one and two sometime," said Houlihan.

"And during this time had you had anything to eat?"

"No."

"Alright, and then what happened?"

"Then he said, 'I'm not going to waste a lot of time with you, Houlihan. We've got the proof. We can just as easily send this case to trial and when you're convicted you'll get the death penalty. Hacking off the victim's head will do it. But for fifteen minutes I'll give you a chance to tell us your side of the story, and there's a good chance you'll escape the death penalty. They don't give the death penalty to people who have confessed.'"

"Are these the detective's exact words?"

"Pretty close. It was a shock to me what he was saying and I remember it pretty well."

"Go on."

"I told him, or started to tell him, that I didn't do it, but he cut me off, shouting at me, 'Don't bullshit me, Houlihan.' So I basically just shut up. There wasn't any point in saying anything."

"And then?"

"He just stayed in the room, standing and staring at me for maybe another ten minutes, and then he left, went out of the room."

"Alright," said Dure.

"So I was left alone in the room for a long time. There was no clock, but I had my cell phone. So I surfed the web."

"You surfed the web?"

"Yes. There was nothing else to do."

Dure said, "I'm going to ask you this, because the prosecution is sure to: Why didn't you call me or my office or someone for help?"

"I don't know. Maybe I didn't think of it. Maybe I was afraid to because they would overhear me. I don't know."

"Okay, go on."

"It was about two hours later, the policeman who had brought me to the police station came in. He said he was sorry he had left me so long, but just after he had brought me in, he had been called out on an emergency call. He had just gotten back."

Houlihan paused as if waiting for Dure to ask him the next question, but Dure was standing behind the defense table, head down, as if lost in thought. After a moment, Houlihan continued on his own initiative:

"So he says to me, 'I understand that Detective Johanssen came in?' 'A detective came in, he didn't tell me his name,' I said. 'Yeah,' he said, 'Johanssen is kinda rough – not rough physically, but he just doesn't like to waste time. So, I'm sorry you had to deal with him.' Then he told me that the police had a surveillance video recording that showed me driving into the development around the time of the crime, and a witness who would testify that I had dragged something heavy and bulky into the back yard. I knew they couldn't have that, so I asked him to show the video to me. He said they couldn't show it to me because it would compromise their witness and their investigation, but that if I went to trial I would see it then."

"They told you they had a video of you?" asked Dure.

"Yes."

"Go on."

"He told me the police did not have any doubt that I killed my wife, and that in his experience with investigations there usually was an explanation for what appeared on the surface to be bad, but usually was done for an understandable reason. So he said if he could get my side of the story, he could probably help me get a favorable plea-bargain for a lesser offense than first-degree murder."

"What was your mental and physical condition at the time?" asked Dure.

"I was getting hungry, and I was tired, and maybe I was still a little woozy from the crash."

"Alright. Please go on."

"I was there for a long time, and the policemen would come in and out of the room, and leave me along for a long time and I'm sure I can't remember everything. But they kept trying to get me to say that I had killed her because of domestic abuse and that that would be a mitigating factor, and they had talked to witnesses who said they thought my wife had been abusive."

"How long did the police hold you?"

"Basically forever, because after I gave them the confession they wanted, they then put me in a cell, and I've been in jail ever since."

"I meant, how long did they hold you before they got you to sign the confession?"

"I think it was around 5:00 in the morning," said Houlihan.

"Five o'clock in the morning!" said Dure.

"Yes, sir."

"Without then asking you to go through every minute of the time, did anything else of importance occur while you were being held?"

"As I remember, the thing that really made me decide to agree to what they wanted was they said if I didn't do it, then it had to have been my son."

"You have a son?"

"Yes, sir. My son Liam. He's 23 years old."

"And where does he live?"

"He lives on University Avenue here in town."

"He does not live at your house?"

"No, he's grown up and moved out."

"Did the police tell you that if you did not confess, they would charge your son with the murder?"

"Objection!" called out prosecutor Preston, rising to his feet. "Counsel is leading the witness."

"Sustained," said the judge. "But since there's no jury, I as judge know when counsel is leading the witness, and it makes the testimony less credible. Not all of us judges are idiots, you know."

"What did the police tell you?" said Dure.

"They said that if I insisted that I didn't do it, then it had to have been my son."

"What about the surveillance video and the eyewitness?"

"They said that my appearance and my son's were similar enough that it could have been either one of us."

"Is your appearance similar to your son's?"

"I suppose, except that he is more fit and weighs less than I do."

"Go on."

Houlihan shrugged his shoulders and looked unhappy. "They were so insistent and so confident and it never occurred to me that the police would lie . . . and I guess I was tired . . . and old, and what do I care about my used-up life compared to the life of my son?"

"This may be my last question. Why are you now recanting your confession?"

"Because it is not true and because you showed me that due to this false confession the police would stop their investigation, and the killer is still out there. Which seems to have come true."

"I have no further questions, Your Honor," said Dure.

Prosecutor Preston stood.

"Mr. Houlihan, you are 51 years old, is that not right?"

"Yes, sir."

"You graduated from high school?"

"Yes."

"You attended two years of college?"

"Yes."

"Do you vote?"

"Sometimes."

"Do you consider yourself a normal, intelligent adult?"

"I guess so."

"Yes or no, do you consider yourself a normal, intelligent adult?"

"Yes."

"You are self-employed?"

"Yes."

"You don't have any boss telling you what to do?"

"No."

"And yet, you have been able to make a living by your own efforts?"

"I suppose."

"It's true, isn't it?"

Houlihan's head swayed back and forth. "Between my wife's income and mine, we were able to pay our bills."

"This confession that you gave, no one physically forced your hand to write your name, isn't that right?"

"Yes."

"And no one struck you or offered any kind of violence?"

"No."

"You know about your Miranda rights, do you not?"

"What do you mean?"

"When you were first questioned, at the time of the initial police investigation, you were given your Miranda rights, were you not?"

"Yes."

"So you had already been advised of those rights at the time you crashed your truck?"

"Not at that time."

"But, before. Before that, you had been advised of your rights?"

"Okay."

"And therefore, you knew of them at that time?"

"At the time of the crash, I was shook up a bit. I wasn't thinking about . . . the murder or rights or anything else."

"You weren't so 'shook up' that you wanted to go to the hospital for treatment. In fact, you specifically and knowingly declined treatment."

"Yes."

"At the time you gave the confession which we have recorded on videotape, and signed the typed transcript of your words, you were not sick?"

"Not more than what I have already said?"

"Oh. You mean you were tired and hungry?"

"And I might have been woozy from the accident."

"You might have been woozy from the accident," repeated Preston in a mocking tone. "We'll see how woozy you were. – If it please the court, I would now like to play for the court the videotaped confession of the defendant, so that I can question him about it."

"Does the defense have any objection?" asked the judge.

"No, Your Honor," said Dure.

"Go ahead, Mr. Preston."

Preston signaled to his associate, Ms. Tinder, who tapped several keys on a computer at the prosecution's table. On the computer screens mounted at the bench, the witness stand, and on counsel's tables, came the image of a police detective and Houlihan in a small room. The video recording showed the detective reading the Miranda warnings, followed by Houlihan's confession. Houlihan had bags under his eyes, and a salt-and-pepper "five o'clock shadow," but otherwise appeared in good condition.

"Was that an accurate depiction of the events which occurred?" asked Preston.

Houlihan admitted that it was.

"I move the admission of this videotape into evidence," said Preston.

"I object, Your Honor," said Dure, getting to his feet. "The whole point of this motion is that the confession should be suppressed and not come into evidence."

"Just for purposes of this hearing," interjected Preston quickly.

"It shouldn't come in for any purpose," said Dure.

"Gentlemen," said the judge. Then addressing the court reporter the judge asked if she had taken down the words of confession as the video had played. The court reporter said that she had. "So, what I'm going to do," said the judge, "is deny the admission of the videotape. The transcription will be in the record of this hearing, but if I grant the motion, I will order the transcription stricken from the record."

Preston resumed his questioning.

"Now Mr. Houlihan, isn't it a fact that the police never told you that they had surveillance video and an eyewitness? Isn't it true that the detective said '*Suppose* I tell you that we had a surveillance video.'?"

"I don't remember his exact words. He definitely gave me the impression that he was claiming to have a surveillance video. That's why I asked to see it."

"Where were you on the afternoon of June 5?"

"Objection!" This question brought Dure to his feet. "Your Honor, this is not a trial on the merits, and the question is irrelevant to the issue here, which is police coercion of a confession."

"Your Honor," said Preston, "the defense is claiming that the confession is a false confession. That means that the facts in the confession are put in issue. If the prosecution can show that Mr. Houlihan is guilty, that defeats the defense's claim that the confession is false."

"If it please the Court," said Dure, "the issue here is police tactics coercing a confession. Even if the confession were true, if it was obtained by coercive methods, it should be suppressed. So this motion does not put the accuracy of the confession in issue. The prosecution is making an unfair attempt to hijack this hearing for discovery purposes."

"I am going to sustain the objection," said the judge. "At the trial, if there is a trial, the question of guilt or innocence will be thoroughly litigated."

"You voluntarily accompanied Corporal Snyder to the station?" asked Preston.

"The reason I got in his car is that he said he was going to give me a ride home."

Preston seemed embarrassed by this answer. "But when Corporal Snyder suggested going to the station, you didn't object at all, did you?

"I wanted to help the police find who murdered my wife. . . . And besides, I did not think it would be intelligent to jump out of a moving police car."

"Isn't it true that you could have left the police station at any time?"

"I didn't think so."

"It is true that at no time did any police officer tell you that you were under arrest?"

"I can't remember."

"And in fact, you never asked to leave?"

"I didn't think that I would be allowed to leave."

"You never asked to leave?"

"No."

"I have no further questions," said Preston.

"Does the defense wish to re-direct?" asked the judge.

"No, Your Honor," said Dure.

The defendant has just left the stand, typed Bornstein. *The defense made some good points, including that the police appeared to initiate the conversation about the crime and did not give a Miranda warning at that time, and that the police appear to have held the defendant unreasonably long without sleep or food, and may have misled him about the facts. One of the most important things brought out was a threat made by the police to charge the defendant's son if the defendant did not confess. The prosecution did not address this fact on cross-examination. But the prosecution otherwise did a good job on cross, showing that the defendant is a normal, mature, functioning adult who was aware of his Miranda rights. Further, the prosecution threw into question whether the defendant was in custody at all, certainly opening the door to the possibility that his presence and statements at the police station were all voluntary. I'm going to score this advantage defense, but not a large advantage.* [post]

Dure next called Police Corporal Roger Snyder to testify. A tall, physically fit man, balding, and wearing a mustache, took the witness stand. After some preliminaries, Dure asked:

"So what I understand is that you were part of the team that investigated the scene of death on June 5, and that you responded on June 15 to the report of the vehicle crash. At the crash site, you recognized Mr. Houlihan from your having been on the scene on June 5. Is that correct?"

"Yes, sir."

"You investigated the scene of the crime on June 5?"

"Yes."

"You were one of the initial responders to the scene?"

"Yes."

"Before you were notified to respond to the nine Cherry Lane address, the police had no notice of a potential homicide at that address?"

"Not as far as I know."

"You arrived at the crime scene shortly before noon?"

"As I recall, it was about 11:47 a.m."

"The chief investigator on this case was Lt. Wisdom, isn't that right?"

"Yes."

"What time did Lt. Wisdom arrive at the scene?"

"It was around 12:30."

"When you got to the scene, Mr. Houlihan met you, didn't he?"

"Yes."

"And his first words to you were, 'There's a body in the back yard. I'm afraid it might be my wife,' or words to that effect?"

"I've brought my notebook with me. Is it alright if I consult my notes?"

"Please do."

Corporal Snyder unbuttoned the flap on the left front pocket of his uniform shirt and withdrew a small notebook. He paged in it briefly and said, "He said, 'Officer, there's something in the back yard that looks like a body, and I'm afraid it might be my wife.' That's reasonably close to an exact quote because I made this note that day at the scene."

"He did not say to you, 'It is my wife'?"

Preston got to his feet and objected. The two attorneys approached the bench and spoke in whispers with the judge. The court reporter picked up his machine with its stand and stood with the attorneys to take down the colloquy.

"Your Honor has already ruled that this is not a hearing on the merits and that the accuracy of the confession is not in issue," said Preston. "Yet here is Mr. Dure going into matters that have nothing to do with the giving of the confession or the manner in which it was obtained. I object on the grounds of relevance and waste of time."

"What have you got to say to that, Mr. Dure?" said the judge.

"What I am seeking to put before the Court with this evidence," said Dure, "is the universe of suspects which the police considered. This has bearing on how the police chose to concentrate their suspicion on Mr. Houlihan, to the neglect of other suspects, and this then bears on why they would seek to induce Mr. Houlihan to confess."

"I think I see your point," said the judge, "but I also think it is rather attenuated. I'm going to sustain the objection. Get on with the main issue, Mr. Dure."

As the conference disbanded Preston gave Dure an aristocratic smirk as if to say, 'Gotcha with your own argument. Hah!'

Dure was irked.

The participants returned to their places.

"Corporal Snyder," said Dure, "let me direct your attention to the 15th of June, and specifically to your responding to a call to investigate a report of a vehicle crash. Now you testified that you recognized Mr. Houlihan from having investigated the homicide scene, isn't that right?"

"Yes."

"And you recognized Mr. Houlihan right away, isn't that right?"

"I don't know what you mean."

"As soon as you saw Mr. Houlihan, you recognized him from your investigation only ten days before, isn't that right?"

"I recognized him."

"You did not consult your notebook, did you?"

"No."

"And you did not ask Mr. Houlihan who he was?"

"I don't recall doing so."

"In fact, you recognized him right away?"

Corporal Snyder shrugged. "I suppose if you want to put it that way."

"So from the first moment you arrived at that scene, you regarded your involvement as part of the murder investigation, not as a mere investigation of a vehicle accident?"

"I can't say that."

"You don't deny it."

"It's not a question that I thought about. As a police officer, you have to be always alert."

"At some point during your investigation, you offered Mr. Houlihan a ride to his home?"

"I did."

"Over the course of, let's say, the past two years, how many vehicle accident investigations have you been involved in?"

Corporal Snyder shrugged his shoulders. "I'd say, maybe, I don't know, a hundred."

"And of these, say, hundred investigations, on how many occasions did you offer to give the person involved in the accident a ride home?"

Corporal Snyder, could see where this line of questions was going. In a defiant manner he said, "I don't recall any."

"It was only on this one occasion, with Mr. Houlihan, that you offered to give the driver a ride home."

"That's right." The tone of voice said, So what?

"During your investigation at the scene, you had conversation with Mr. Houlihan?"

"I don't know what you mean by 'conversation.' I spoke to him, and he spoke to me, if that's what you mean."

"You noticed that he was dazed and disoriented after the crash?"

"I'm not a doctor."

"Do you mean to say that only a doctor is capable of noticing whether someone is dazed and disoriented?"

"I don't know."

"You don't know what you meant to say?"

"I'm not going to let you twist my words."

"Twist your words? I asked you straightforwardly whether you noticed that Mr. Houlihan was dazed and disoriented after the crash. You did not say 'yes'; you did not say 'no.' You said 'I'm not a doctor.' Who's twisting words?"

Corporal Snyder did not answer.

"I didn't hear your answer," said Dure.

"What was the question?" said Corporal Snyder.

"Since I think everyone in the courtroom knows what the answer to my question is, I won't repeat it. I'll go back to my original question, which for some reason you do not want to answer: Didn't you notice that Mr. Houlihan was dazed and disoriented after the crash?"

"No."

"Didn't you in fact, urge him to go with the medics to the hospital to get checked out?"

"He insisted he was okay and didn't want to go to the hospital."

"Didn't you in fact, urge him to go with the medics to the hospital to get checked out? I'd like you to answer the question."

"I may have said something to that effect."

"You may have said something. I take it from that that you do not have a clear recollection of the events of that occasion."

"That's not a question."

"Do you disagree with my assertion that you do not have a clear recollection of the events of that occasion?"

"Yes."

"So you do have a clear recollection?"

"Yes."

"And in your clear recollection, you did or did not urge Mr. Houlihan to go with the medics to get checked out?"

"I did, because that's just routine in such cases. Whether or not the individual shows any symptoms."

"But in this particular case, Mr. Houlihan appeared dazed and disoriented?"

"He was lucid and normal."

"So now, you're a doctor."

"No."

"Just a minute ago, you implied that only a doctor can tell if someone is dazed and disoriented. Now you are telling us that you noticed that he was not dazed and disoriented, but was lucid and normal. Doesn't that require exactly the same kind of observation?"

"No. Anybody can tell whether an individual is acting normally, but to diagnose dazed and disoriented for certain requires a doctor."

"So you can tell if someone is not dazed and disoriented, but you can't tell if someone is dazed and disoriented?"

"Right."

"Sort of like you can tell if someone is guilty, but you can't tell if they're innocent."

"Actually, yes."

"Alright now, Doctor Snyder, still directing --"

"Objection!" Preston was on his feet. He put on his most outraged manner. "Your Honor! Mr. Dure knows this is *Corporal* Snyder. His sarcastic misappellation is disrespectful to the witness."

"Sustained," said the judge.

Some good cross-examination going on, typed Bornstein. Typically, police officers are experienced witnesses who are difficult to cross-examine. But Mr. Dure is not letting this officer get away with being evasive. On the issue whether Mr. Houlihan was disoriented after the crash of his truck, the two battled pretty much to a draw. The officer finally testified that Houlihan was lucid and normal, but the force of this testimony was essentially destroyed by the officer's preceding evasiveness. We will see if the witness will be more cooperative after this jousting. However, Dure overplayed his hand by referring to the officer as 'Doctor.' The judge sustained the prosecutor's objection, and now, every time Dure refers to the witness as 'Corporal,' it will seem like a defeat for him. [post]

"Excuse me," said Dure, "Corporal Snyder. Still directing your attention to your investigation of the crash on June 15, you said to Mr. Houlihan in the course of your conversation with him words to the effect of, 'You're the man whose wife was murdered over in Sunderly Chase?'?"

"Something to that effect."

"Before you said that, Mr. Houlihan had said nothing about that subject?"

"Not that I recall."

"And you have a clear recollection of the investigation?"

"Yes." Corporal Snyder answered curtly, and looked away from Dure and down, as if he didn't want to admit the answer.

"You were the first one to raise that subject?"

"As far as I recall.

"And you have a clear recollection of the investigation?"

"Yes." Corporal Snyder answered again curtly, as if he were tired of the question.

"And before you asked that question of Mr. Houlihan, you did not give him any Miranda warning, isn't that right?"

"No."

"No, it's not right, or no, you did not give him any warning?"

"No, I did not mirandize him at that time."

"Mr. Houlihan told you, that yes, he was the man whose wife had been murdered?"

"Yes."

"And at that time, after he told you he was the man, you did not give him any Miranda warning?"

"No."

"Now you told us that you participated in the initial investigation of the murder on June 5, isn't that right?"

"Yes." Corporal Snyder answered slowly.

"As of the end of that day, the first day of the investigation, you, that is, the police, had only one suspect, namely, Mr. Houlihan?"

"He was a suspect."

"In fact, at that time, he was the only suspect?"

"I can't say that. Other officers were involved in the investigation."

"As far as you knew, Mr. Houlihan was the only suspect at that time?"

"No, At that time, *everybody* was a suspect."

Dure paused. "At the time, therefore, when you were investigating the truck crash, Mr. Houlihan was a suspect in the unsolved crime of his wife's murder?"

"Yes."

"At the time, when you were investigating the truck crash, you knew Mr. Houlihan was a suspect in the unsolved crime of his wife's murder?"

"Yes."

"In fact, at the time, when you were investigating the truck crash, as far as you knew, Mr. Houlihan was the only identified suspect in the unsolved crime of his wife's murder?"

The corporal swayed his head from side to side as if trying to decide a difficult point. "Yes," he said reluctantly.

"At the time, therefore, when you initiated a discussion of the unsolved crime of his wife's murder, you knew Mr. Houlihan was a suspect in the case?"

"Yes."

"And at the time when you initiated a discussion of the unsolved crime of his wife's murder, knowing that

Mr. Houlihan was a suspect in the case, you did not give him a Miranda warning?"

"No, I did not. I wasn't concerned because I knew that he had already had his Miranda rights read to him."

"You weren't concerned . . . meaning that you thought about the matter and decided, 'nah, I'm not going to give him Miranda rights today.'?"

"No, I just knew I didn't have to worry about it because he had already had his rights read to him."

"So you decided not to read him his rights on this occasion when you initiated a discussion about the unsolved murder in which Mr. Houlihan was a suspect?"

"Again, it wasn't a conscious decision, it was just something that I didn't have to worry about."

"After you asked Mr. Houlihan if he were the man whose wife had been murdered, he told you that he was, isn't that right?"

"Yes, or words to that effect."

"And then you offered him a ride to his home?"

"At some point I did."

"And he accepted and got in your car?"

"At some time, yes."

"And you drove off in the direction of Mr. Houlihan's home?"

"Yes."

"You knew the location of Mr. Houlihan's home because you had been present at the investigation on June 5th?"

"Yes."

"And so you drove off in that direction."

"Yes."

"And then you said to him, 'You could help us clear up a few point if you'd be willing to come down to the station.'?"

"I said something to that effect, I don't remember the exact words."

"It wasn't until after Mr. Houlihan was in the patrol car that you said this to him?"

"I'm not sure whether it was before or after he got in the car."

"You testified earlier that you had a clear recollection of this investigation."

"Okay."

"Now if you had suggested going to the station before Mr. Houlihan got in the car, then you would have driven off towards the station from the get-go, rather than in the direction of Mr. Houlihan's home?"

"From the location of the crash, it was the same direction to them both, at least from the road we were on."

"You testified that you drove off in the direction of Mr. Houlihan's home, meaning that at the instant when you began to drive, your intent was to go to Mr. Houlihan's home, isn't that right?"

"They were in the same direction."

"You did not answer my question. At the time you first drove away from the crash site, you were driving to Mr. Houlihan's home, isn't that right?"

"If you want to put that construction on it."

"Well, it's not the case that you told Mr. Houlihan that you would give him a ride home, and then, when he got in the car you right away intended to drive to the station, was it?"

"No."

"Because that would be outright deception, and you would not do that, right?"

"No."

"And so it was after Mr. Houlihan got in the car that you suggested going to the station instead of to his home?"

Corporal Snyder said, "Yeah," and shrugged his shoulders.

The judge interrupted: "Counsel, it's getting on towards the lunch hour. How much longer do you think you'll be with this witness?"

"Your Honor, I think I'm going to hang out my shingle as a dentist, because I'm pulling teeth this morning. However, I only have one more to go, and it's not a wisdom tooth. I shouldn't be more than a few minutes if the witness is even a little bit cooperative."

"I'm not sure I would count on that," said the judge. "But go ahead. Try to get done by noon."

Dure nodded to the judge. Then he went to the defense table and whispered with Houlihan. Turning back to address the witness, he said, "You drove along Creek Road towards downtown, isn't that right?"

"Yes, sir."

"The turn-off into Sunderly Chase is a left turn from Creek Road when driving towards town, right?"

"Yes."

"When you got to the turn-off, you did not turn left into Sunderly Chase, but sailed on by, saying at that time, 'Why don't you come down to the station and maybe help us clear up a couple of questions?'?"

"I . . . can't remember the exact timing."

"You then cannot deny that you suggested to Mr. Houlihan to go with you to the station as you were passing by the entrance to Sunderly Chase?"

Corporal Snyder shrugged his shoulders again. "Could be, I don't know."

"You don't deny it?"

"I suppose not."

"Do you deny it?"

"No."

"And once you had driven by the entrance to Sunderly Chase, Mr. Houlihan was essentially in custody."

"I disagree."

"The car was traveling at 35 or 40 miles per hour?"

"About."

"And Mr. Houlihan could not get out of a moving car, could he?"

"Not while it was moving, no."

"No further questions."

Bornstein typed, *The defense has gone a long way toward establishing a key point, that the defendant was in custody at the time he gave his confession.* [post]

***

After lunch, Prosecutor Preston, cross-examining Corporal Snyder, got him to testify that Houlihan was sitting in the front seat of the car; that in the front seat, the inside door handles worked; that Houlihan could have exited the vehicle at any traffic light where the car stopped; that if Houlihan had asked, Corporal Snyder would have turned around and taken him home.

After that, the judge seemed to become less patient. He began to sustain all kinds of objections, and hurried the lawyers on. The lawyers did their best to "move things along," not wanting to irritate the judge. The examinations of Detective Johanssen and Lt. Wisdom were conducted with dispatch; the judge even admonished the detective to "stop playing games and answer the questions."

"I will hear brief argument," said the judge, when the lawyers announced that they had no further witnesses.

"May it please the court," began Dure. "You have heard that Mr. Houlihan has no criminal record. Thus, he is not familiar with the police and how they work, is not familiar with the inside of a police car or the police station. For someone like Mr. Houlihan, the police are intimidating. Being inside a police car is intimidating, not to mention being inside a police interrogation room. Even supposing that the police would have released him had he asked to be set free, the intimidation factor prevented him from presuming such a liberty with the authority of the police. And as Your Honor has seen from the testimony from the witness stand, police officers have an authoritative presence and a keen sense of practical psychology. Thus, in effect, and for practical purposes, Mr. Houlihan was in custody while he was being questioned by the police.

"Moreover, once at the police station, Mr. Houlihan was dependent on the police to give him a ride home, and thus was in effect held at the police's pleasure.

"Since Mr. Houlihan was in custody, the police were required to give him the Miranda warnings. Now such warnings were given obviously and prominently in the video recording which Your Honor saw, but it is improper for the police to question a suspect, get the confession they want, and then give Miranda warnings just before recording the suspects repetition of the confession. And Your Honor heard Corporal Snyder testify that he brought up the subject of the crime first, at the scene of the accident, and that he did not give a Miranda warning at that time.

"The testimony of the police about other warnings given at the station is self-serving, vague, and in some respects contradictory. There is a growing trend in law enforcement to record the entire interrogation, so that there can be no doubt about the giving of Miranda warnings, not to mention the fair conduct of the interrogation altogether, but that was not done here. The Court should therefore view with some skepticism the testimony of the police about Miranda warnings."

Dure bent down to consult his notes.

"The question thus for the Court to determine is: did the police coerce Mr. Houlihan into this confession? Fairly viewing the facts, the answer is 'yes.'

"First of all, they made false claims about the evidence they had. Now Det. Johanssen argued that he told no lies because he did not say he had a surveillance recording and a witness, but merely that he said '*Suppose* I told you that we have . . ..' This is a transparent sophistry. Your Honor would not let the attorneys who appear before you get away with lying to the Court through such a stratagem.

"A police officer is a state official. A person in authority. When such a person represents that he has certain evidence, this assertion, objectively speaking, must compel belief.

"Next, the police promised leniency to Mr. Houlihan if he would confess. They said he could get the death penalty if he did not confess. Given the imperfections of the justice system, this is something that even an innocent person has to consider as a realistic possibility. And a promise, or even a suggestion that a suspect can avoid being put to death by confessing must be considered, again on an objective basis, as heavy coercion.

"Finally, and most egregiously, the police threatened to – really, in effect, to put Mr. Houlihan's son to death if he did not confess. As you have heard, they told him that they would arrest and prosecute his son if he continued to claim that he did not do it. To arrest and prosecute someone for murder is to intend to put that person to death. This is such a strong coercive factor, that it alone should invalidate this confession."

Prosecutor Preston now stood to address the court.

"Your honor, we have spent a whole day on what really is a desperate attempt by the defense to deprive the Court and the jury, should it come to that, of the most important, and most credible evidence on the issue of who committed this gruesome murder, and that is the statement of the defendant himself.

"The defense has fluffed up a mountain of words, but they cannot obscure the fact that the defendant is a mature, self-sufficient man, experienced in the world, married for years, having raised a son, and operated his own business. Therefore, it is absurd to claim that he could not tell the police that he wanted to leave whenever he wanted. I submit to the court that it was not the supposedly great authority of the police's manner that held him, but rather the fear induced by guilt, and the subconscious desire that all the guilty have to confess. You heard all three of the police witnesses testify that Mr. Houlihan was not under arrest, he was not cuffed, he could have left anytime he wanted.

"As Mr. Dure has admitted, the police did not lie to the defendant about the evidence, they merely proposed a hypothetical statement that would worry only someone who was guilty, someone who knew that such evidence might exist, because in fact he did the things that the evidence would have shown. So this is a non-issue.

"As to the supposed threat by the police to put Mr. Houlihan's son to death if he did not confess, this is hyperbole of the grossest kind. I would say that it is born of desperation. No one has ever heard of such a thing. But to point out to a suspect that the perpetrator can likely be only one of two people is merely laying cards on the table. Coercion it is not."

Bornstein was tapping away. *Attorney Dure has put on a good case, making three powerful points: the false claims by the police of having inculpatory evidence; the promise of leniency; and the threat to go after the defendant's son if the defendant did not confess. The cumulative effect of all three of these factors could well amount to coercion, that is, an overbearing of the defendant's will by police pressure. The weak point in Dure's case is whether the defendant really was in custody, or whether his presence at the police station was voluntary. The judge could go either way on this, but given the powerful evidence of coercion, it would not be surprising if the judge tossed the confession.* [post]

"In closing, I want to draw the Court's attention to a remarkable parallel between Mr. Houlihan's confession and his testimony in court today. In his confession, he says that he cannot remember what he did with the head and with the murder weapon. At first blush, this might seem strange. But now, in his testimony today, here right before the Court, he testified that with regard to the accident on June 15, he cannot recall what happened just before and during the crash. I suggest to the Court, that Mr. Houlihan has a mental condition, or maybe it is a moral frailty, pursuant to which he blocks from his mind his acts of great culpability. I submit to the Court that Mr. Houlihan's testimony in court today bolsters the credibility of his confession."

The prosecutor has just made a powerful point as well, pointing out a parallel between the defendant's failure of memory in his confession and his failure of memory in today's court testimony. County Attorney Preston is no slouch. If the confession does not get tossed, then I expect we'll hear this same argument at trial. [post]

"Mr. Houlihan voluntarily accompanied Corporal Snyder to the police station where he voluntarily spoke with the police about the murder of his wife. He was not arrested, he was not handcuffed, he was not told that he was under arrest. He could have left at any time. There was no coercion by the police. I request Your Honor to deny the defense's motion."

"Thank you, counsel," said the judge. "The motion will be denied. I will give you a written ruling in a couple of days. Court is adjourned."

Dure showed no reaction to the court's ruling, but quietly closed the books on the defense table, gathered up has papers, and squared them into a neat pile.

While he had been doing this, the sheriff's deputies had come up to Houlihan and were hovering one on each side of him, preparing to put him in handcuffs again.

Dure turned to Houlihan. The pupils in Dure's light hazel eyes were contracted into pinpoints. "We are not done," he said. The metal bracelets clicked as Houlihan's arms were held behind his back. The sheriff's deputies held him gently by the arms and steered him towards the access door in the front of the courtroom.

Preston was speaking in a low voice with his associate Ms. Tinder. As Dure passed through the gate from the well of the court he overheard her say, "After this, what choice do they have? They've got to come to us for a deal."

10.

"What I can't believe," said Dure, as he discussed the case with Kara and Ralph in Dure's office, "is that for two, or even three days, nobody in that neighborhood saw anything. How does a woman get killed, her body put in the back yard, vultures coming and going, and nobody notices anything? – for three days! Does that seem reasonable? Maybe there's a conspiracy of the whole neighborhood against the Houlihans. They murder *her*, pin it on her *husband*, and get rid of the whole family!"

"Then maybe the kid's in danger," said Kara.

"What?" said Dure.

"Never mind," said Kara.

"But motive?" said Dure. "What could the motive be?"

" 'member?" said Ralph. "That woman across the street said she was a terror to the neighborhood?"

Dure made a wry face. "We need to re-interview the neighbors. We're missing something. We need to re-interview them after we get as complete a background as we can get." He picked up the phone and called Kurt Kniffe.

"Kurt? I want you to find out everything you can about the immediate neighbors of the Houlihans: how long they've lived there, what they do for a living, the clubs they belong to, everything. Check the court records about any lawsuits, see if you can find any records of police arrests. See what information you can get from the homeowners' association. The point is, somebody there had to see, or hear, or, for crying out loud, even smell something, and why aren't they talking?"

A chime sounded. Kara got up and left the room.

"Can you get it to me by Friday?" said Dure, still on the telephone. "I know, but trial begins in eleven days." Dure hung up.

Kara returned carrying a large manila envelope. "This was hand-carried from the County Attorney's office," she said as she handed it to Dure.

Dure opened it. Inside were some twenty or so sheets of paper. "Brady materials," he said. He began to look through them. "I wonder why they did not give us this earlier," he said. His eyes ran rapidly over first page; he slipped it aside, scanned the second, and continued, spending no more than five seconds per page. After having shucked eleven sheets of paper onto his desk, he dwelt for a moment on the twelfth. He glanced up at the ceiling for a moment, then said, "This might be of interest. The police interviewed the wife of Rhys Parker."

"A jealous wife?" Kara mused.

"If Parker was involved with Mrs. Houlihan, his wife would seem to be within a reasonable circle of suspects," said Dure.

"Even if Parker wasn't diddling the Houlihan woman," said Ralph, "maybe his wife thought he was."

"This report is vague," said Dure, "and I'm guessing that the police did not follow up because once Houlihan confessed, they were done with the case. Something's odd here." He gave the sheet to Kara. "Please make a copy . . . also, a subpoena for Dawn Parker – the spelling of the name is on this page . . . make it for the second day of the trial."

Kara took the paper and left the office.

"Ralph, I'll want you to serve the subpoena. Let's do it now."

Ralph nodded and left the office to get the car from the garage. Eight minutes later Kara brought Dure a copy of the page from the supplemental police report that he had requested, a subpoena form with the proper blanks filled in, and lastly, a sheet of paper listing the address of Mr. Parker's real estate brokerage and his home address.

Dure checked them over and signed the subpoena form. "Good job," he said, making a small smile without parting his lips. He so rarely smiled that Kara was surprised and felt pleased.

Ralph had Dure's car waiting at the curb in front of the office. Dure got in the passenger's seat and handed the paper with the address to Ralph, who punched the office address into the car's GPS.

The office of Parker Realty was in a neat strip mall of five or six store fronts. Large panes of plate glass fronted on a shallow parking lot. Ralph pulled the car into the middle space of three empty spaces right in front of the office. In the bright sunlight, the glass front of the office reflected a Technicolor image of the two men getting out of the car.

A beep sounded as they went through the door into what turned out to be an empty reception area. Other than that quick beep, the office was silent. Dure and Ralph stood waiting, observing. After more than enough time had passed for someone to come out and greet them, Dure called out a 'hello.' Still no one responded and it appeared as if the office were unoccupied. Yet that seemed unlikely as the front door was not locked.

To their left were two small, glass-fronted conference rooms. Inside each were a small, round table and three chairs. The doors to these rooms stood half open, no one was in them, and there were no papers on the tables.

"Hello! Is anyone here?" called out Dure, louder this time.

Dure stood at the reception desk, looking at what was on it without touching anything. Ralph ventured to enter the half-dark hallway to the right of the reception desk.

A woman shrieked and Ralph jumped as she nearly collided with him. "Sorry!" said Ralph.

"I didn't know anyone was here," said the woman, holding her hand to her chest as if to still her heart.

Ralph backed up and the woman came out into the reception area. "Can I help you?" she said. She wore a professional-looking skirt and blouse. As she stood expecting an answer or explanation from these two men, she fidgeted with one hand about the top of her skirt, seeming to try to adjust an undergarment.

"I'm looking for Dawn Parker," said Dure.

"That's me," she said. "How can I help you?"

"Here's my card," he said.

She took it and Dure waited until she had looked at it. When she looked up, he said, "I'd like to talk with you about the Houlihan case. You're familiar with it?"

"I've heard about it, but I don't know anything about it," she said.

"Did you know Mrs. Houlihan?"

Her manner became wary. "No," she said. She moved over to the reception desk and put Dure's card on it, as if she were done with it and him.

"But you knew who she was?" said Dure.

At this her eyes flashed. "I'm sorry, I have work to do. You'll excuse me," she said, by way of indicating that the interview was over.

Dure nodded to Ralph, who took the folded subpoena from his back pocket and gave it to Mrs. Parker.

"What's this?" she said.

"A subpoena," said Dure.

She unfolded the paper and looked at it. Ralph stepped to a chair, sat down, and began to fill in the service affidavit on his copy of the subpoena.

Mrs. Parker looked seriously unhappy. "Why don't you leave me alone," she said.

"If you'll talk with me now, I may be able to determine that I don't need you to testify at trial, and I could rescind the subpoena. I don't guarantee that, but if you don't want to talk now, I can guarantee that you'll have to answer questions in court and under oath."

She stood with her arms crossed, breathing angrily, her jaw clenched. "Lawyers," she said with disgust.

Dure said nothing. His dark gray suit was unfashionably roomy, as if perhaps he had lost weight. No smile played about his lips; the only feature in his face that showed any sign of life was his light eyes, focusing on her as if they were tractor beams.

"Alright, let's sit in here," she said, forcing herself between Dure and the reception desk, almost shoving him out of the way, and going into one of the small conference rooms.

Ralph joined them and the three chairs in the small room were all occupied. "The police talked with you," said Dure.

She nodded.

"What did you tell them?" asked Dure.

"Basically that I didn't know anything."

"They were happy with that answer?"

"What choice did they have?"

"They have ways," said Dure. "What I'd be interested in knowing is what they asked you, why did they want to talk with you?"

"I don't remember. You could ask them."

Dure carried with him a slender leather briefcase. He took from it the copy which Kara had made of the Supplemental Report from the police file. "In fact, I have a copy of the police record of interview," he said. "I'd like to check on the accuracy of this record by comparing what it says with what you say."

"Let me see it," she said.

"If I do that, it would contaminate your memory. I'll show it to you before we leave."

She sighed. Exasperated she blurted out a rapid stream of speech. "They wanted to know as best as I remember where my husband was on the weekend of the murder what his relationship with that woman was and where I was."

"Yes?" said Dure. When she did not respond to this prompt, Dure was more explicit: "What did you tell them?"

The woman was not unattractive. Her shiny brunette hair shimmered in the light as she spoke. "I was showing houses that Friday and Saturday. The police were fully satisfied." She intertwined her fingers and rested her hands and forearms on the table in front of her, a triangular prow like the cowcatcher on a locomotive.

"And your husband?"

"He was doing the same. We were in and out of the office." She was sitting up straight, her jaw subtly thrust forward.

"How well did you know Mrs. Houlihan?"

"Not at all."

"How well did your husband know her?"

"I think they were political buddies," she said. There might have been a note of sarcasm in her voice, or it might have been defiance and resentment towards Dure.

The room darkened slightly, as if the shadow of a shadow had come upon it. Yet it was enough to make Dure turn and look. Through the glass front of the room and the glass front of the office a tall truck could be seen just pulling into a parking space in front of the office.

"I take it," said Dure, turning back, "that you keep some kind of records as to to whom and when you show houses . . ."

"Yes," she said.

". . . so that you could – if it were necessary – give the names of the people to whom you showed houses on that weekend."

"Yes."

"I think," said Dure, "that I won't need you to testify at trial, but that could change. So, we'll leave the subpoena in place, but it is likely that I will let you know before your appearance date that we don't need you."

The woman nodded.

"Thank you for your time," he said.

"I'm glad I could help," she said, but there was heavy irony in her voice.

* * *

Dure and Kniffe met after lunch. The day being sunny and the temperature moderate for July, they decided to walk to the park.

"The immediate neighbors of the Houlihans are three," said Kniffe, beginning to report on his investigation as they walked, "The Vanderlogens on the right, Loveless on the left, and the Sweets across the street."

"What about their neighbors to the back?" asked Dure. They stopped at a corner to wait for traffic to clear before they crossed the street.

"To the rear of the Houlihan residence is an area of uncontrolled arboreous growth, or as they say, a strip of woods," said Kniffe, "I thought you had surveilled the scene?"

"I did," said Dure. "and I assume that behind that strip of woods is another house?" They crossed the street.

"There is. But because that strip of woods is approximately 200 yards wide, and the total distance between the two houses is almost a quarter of a mile, that house is not within the scope of what you asked me to investigate, that being the 'immediate neighbors.'"

"That is fair," said Dure. At the next corner they turned right to go down West Miner Street.

"I did in fact exceed somewhat the scope of the tasked investigation by conducting a discreet inquiry into a fourth residence in the development, but then, I did not want to go beyond that without consulting you first."

"That is well. A fourth residence?"

"The residence of Mr. and Mrs. Parker is in that development, although they are not immediate neighbors of the Houlihans."

"Hmm," said Dure. "I did not connect their street address with that development."

"The connection is not superficially evident," said Kniffe.

"Ah! I see it now. The streets in Sunderly Chase are named after tree species. So it has a Cherry Lane and a Chestnut Lane."

Kniffe half-smiled and nodded.

"Were the developers so specific as to use only the names of fruiting trees?" asked Dure.

"No. There's a Maple Drive . . . although there is also a Walnut Circle."

"Home of the fruits and nuts," said Dure. "All deciduous trees?"

"No, there's a Hemlock Court."

"Never mind," said Dure.

They arrived at the small Baldwin's Grove Park, which was five blocks from Dure's office. Around the perimeter of the park at wide intervals were mature oak trees, three feet in diameter at their base. In the middle of the park, which was flat, open ground, a couple of teenage boys were playing with a Frisbee. The two professional men sat on a bench in the shade.

"The Vanderlogens no one has seen," said Kniffe. "I had an operative stake out the house. He did not observe anyone go in or out. When the lawn mowing crew came, he questioned them. They have a standing order to mow the lawn once a week. The man who mowed the lawn did not know anything about how payment arrangements were made." Kniffe sat with both feet flat on the ground; his lumbar spine followed the curved contour of the park bench and his elbows rested on the back of the bench. "We developed information as to Mr. Vanderlogen's place of employment. They would only say that he is out of the office and are 'not sure' when he will return. None of the neighbors have seen any of the Vanderlogens since the end of May, and the unfalsified hypothesis at the moment is that they went to Holland for a summer vacation. If in fact they left town after school let out in May, that would eliminate them from any suspicion."

Dure sat to Kniffe's right. Dure's right leg was crossed over the other, his right foot pointing off in an oblique direction. While keeping his back straight, his head was bent down in thoughtful concentration and his hands were clasped in his lap. "It also eliminates them from being witnesses who might or might not have been useful," he said.

"Regarding the residence on the other side of the Houlihans," said Kniffe. "Loveless is a retired chemist. He worked at the Cartong Chemical Company. Seventy years old. His wife died ten years ago. No children." Kniffe recited all of these facts without checking any notes or written report. His gaze swept the park as he spoke. "No arrest record. No lawsuits. Member of the Greenback Party. Apparently he used to be a bird-watcher. Caused the proverbial raised eyebrow among the neighbors by walking around the neighborhood with binoculars, but apparently gave up that practice some time ago."

Dure nodded.

"Across the street" said Kniffe. "are the Sweets, Darryl and Doris. Two girls, aged fifteen and seventeen. He is the comptroller at LiveRite Mobile Home Manufacturing. She works part-time at Martel University. No arrest record. No lawsuits. Shortly after the Sweets moved into their house, six years ago, they had put up a political sign in their yard. A day later they got a visit from Mrs. Houlihan who told them it was against the rules and they had to take it down. What Mrs. Sweet remembers about this is that Mrs. Houlihan smiled and was civil, but she made demands like a tyrant. The Sweets *would* take down their sign or there would be consequences."

"Unh-hmm." Dure nodded.

"The homeowner's association does not have an office and is deficient in record-keeping practices. Just meeting minutes and some financial records. We developed a source who had been a long-time member of the council. He knew Mrs. Houlihan as the proverbial squeaky wheel. According to him, she must have kept a copy of the association rules by her bedside. She would complain to the association about other people's signs, flags, long grass . . ." Here Kniffe did reach into the breast pocket of his suit jacket and take out a notebook. ". . . trash containers, RV's in the driveway, curtain linings – "

"Curtain linings?" said Dure.

"In Sunderly Chase, with respect to windows which are visible from the road, the allowable colors for curtain linings are regulated," said Kniffe. He glanced at the next page in his notebook, then put it back in his pocket.

"The implication is," said Dure, "that she made someone in the development change the linings on their curtains?"

"That is the implication from the information we have developed."

"Do you know who it was?"

"No."

"Okay. What else?"

"Here's a lagniappe: As I mentioned, the Parkers also live in this development."

"But they're not immediate neighbors," said Dure.

"No. They live on Locust Lane, about four tenths of a mile away, as the crow flies," replied Kniffe, "but, if you drive, it's about 1.1 miles from the Houlihans'." Kniffe paused, as if annoyed. When Dure did not say anything, and it was clear that Kniffe had the floor, he said, "One of my female investigators belongs to the

Reform Party, and I had her do some checking on this case. Later, as it were, by serendipity, she was talking with a party insider who said there was definitely some extracurricular activity between Tiffany Houlihan and Rhys Parker."

Dure picked up on Kniffe's desire to impress with a juicy story, so he remained quiet and attentive.

"According to this insider, a group of six party activists, including Tiffany Houlihan and Rhys Parker, were having a meeting in a private room in a restaurant. Two bottles of wine were ordered, though it's not clear if they were fully consumed. After the meeting, three people left. The Houlihan woman and Mr. Parker and the party insider remained. He said that Mrs. Houlihan and Mr. Parker quote, got the giggles, and got, quote, googley-eyed, and he became uncomfortable. He left and doesn't know how long the other two stayed there."

Dure nodded as if digesting this information. "So . . . all of that is background. And your men apparently talked at least with Mrs. Sweet . . ."

"Yes."

"Were they able to find out if anyone saw, or heard, or noticed anything during the key weekend?"

"Mrs. Sweet said that when they had found out on Monday about the murder, they were shocked and they all at dinner tried to remember if they had seen anything over the weekend. She said no one could remember anything out of the ordinary and that this frightened them as much as anything, the idea, as she said, that such a thing could happen in the normal course of events."

Not far from where the two men were sitting, a small dog tried to chase a squirrel. The squirrel scampered up the oak tree in the shade of which they were sitting, and the small, white dog tried to follow, fruitlessly rushing a few feet up the trunk, falling back, and yapping in frustration.

"Time is really getting short," said Dure. "I want you to . . ."

Kniffe took out his notebook again.

"Check on the flights of the Vanderlogens. Confirm if they really went on a vacation to Holland, and if so, when they left. Try to interview Loveless and all of the Sweets again, not just Mrs. Sweet. And if possible, interview them separately – I can see how that might be difficult with the two girls – and ask them about *everything* they saw or heard that weekend, not just what might have seemed unusual. Lastly – there are lots of little wooded strips throughout that development, right?"

Kniffe nodded.

"See if there is a path from the Parkers' house to the Houlihans' that goes only through woods. That is, would it be possible to go from one house to the other on foot keeping in the cover of wooded strips?"

Dure steepled his two index fingers and pressed the septum of his nose down on them. His torso oscillated forward and back two or three times. "Okay. That's it. I'll see you later." He put his hands down, rocked his whole body forward, stood up and strode away at a rapid pace, leaving Kniffe behind.

11.

Back in his office, Dure asked Kara to prepare three more subpoenas: a subpoena *duces tecum* for each of Dawn Parker, Rhys Parker, and Parker Real Estate, Inc. requesting the records of house showings for the week of June 3 through June 9.

Then he asked Ralph to serve those subpoenas when Kara had finished preparing them. Finally, he asked Kara to call the jail and set up another interview for him with Mr. Houlihan.

* * *

Yet again Dure went through the gantlet. The dim lighting, the worn condition of all the furniture and fixtures, the way that distrust of everyone was institutionalized and bureaucratized, with sign-in sheets, ID inspection, sitting and waiting, the presence of guards, the clanking and crashing of steel doors and grates.

He and Houlihan went through the Brady materials, which seemed to mean nothing to Houlihan. Then Dure recounted to him the interview with Dawn Parker. This narrative seemed to elicit some form of interest on the part of Houlihan. His formerly shaggy, now shorn, head tilted and twisted, as if he were trying to get a tiny steel ball to fall in the right hole. He pressed together his lips, closed his eyes, and scrunched up his face. "Ah!" he exclaimed, as his head righted itself and his face came back to normal. "That's who it was, Mrs. Parker! She was the woman who avoided me at the gun show!"

Dure was regarding his client with exasperated, skeptical eyes. "Okay . . ." said Dure.

"That could be it," said Houlihan. "She bought a gun at the gun show and shot my wife. I wish I hadn't made that confession."

"Why would she shoot your wife?"

Houlihan's mouth made a moue and he looked up and to his right, staring at the ceiling. "Yeah, I don't know."

Dure had not told everything he had learned or suspected about the possible relationship between Mrs. Houlihan and Mr. Parker. But then, there was that hint in the Brady materials they had just gone over, if one knew what to look for. Had Houlihan picked up on it? Maybe Houlihan did not want to express suspicion of his wife for reasons similar to those which inhibited Dure from mentioning his suspicions to Houlihan: Should a man's life be put in jeopardy for the sake of protecting the memory of an unfaithful wife? Or, was the right question to ask: Should the memory of a faithful wife be ruined for the sake of a far-fetched theory that might not make any difference? There was still a little over a week until trial. Further investigation might make things clearer and decisions easier.

"We were able to listen to Rhys Parker's cell phone," said Dure. "There was what seemed to be a voicemail from your wife at nine thirty on the evening of Friday, June 5. That time is within the outside limits of the broad time frame allowed by the medical examiner for the time of death, but outside of what he considered the most likely time frame. And that's good for you, because to the extent the call suggests that your wife was alive at that time, your alibi is stronger, because you were at the gun show then. When you went looking for alibi witnesses, what time frame were you looking for?"

"At first, the times we discussed, you know, early in the afternoon, as early as possible, to prove I was there at a time that would agree with my having left home when I did. But at the end, I was just looking for anybody who could say I was there, any time."

"You didn't happen to talk with anybody who saw you Friday evening or during the night Friday?"

Houlihan shook his head.

"I said 'seemed to be a voicemail,'" said Dure, "because all we heard was silence for five minutes, or you might call it static. To me, it seemed like a 'pocket dial.' Could that mean anything to you?"

Houlihan shook his head. "As you said, it could have been a pocket dial, or let's see . . . maybe the time stamp got distorted . . . I remember sometimes missing a call, the time would say, maybe one o'clock, but then hours later, the voicemail would come through."

"Did your wife ever call you and then hold the line open without saying anything?"

"No, no."

"But if it was a pocket dial," said Dure, "that would mean that your wife had Mr. Parker's number on her phone. Would you know why that would be?"

"Maybe he called her? About Reform Party business? She did a lot with the Party," said Houlihan.

"One more thing. It seems that your wife vigilant about enforcing various rules in the development: homeowner's association rules, county code . . . I sense that I do not have a complete list of all her activity in this area. Can you give me a run-down of, say, the most recent five years?"

Houlihan was dismissive. "That's nothing," he said, waving his hand down. Houlihan was so evasive that

Dure had to become almost brutal. He slammed him with rapid-fire questions as if he were cross-examining a liar:

"Your wife was killed, right?"

"Your wife was murdered?"

"Someone murdered your wife, isn't that right?"

"You didn't murder your wife, right?"

"If your wife was murdered, and you didn't do it, then someone else did, right?"

"Someone else murdered your wife?"

"You don't know who it was?"

"You don't have any idea who it was?"

"If you don't know who it was, then it could have been anybody?"

"If it could have been anybody, then it could have been one of the neighbors?"

"Or all of the neighbors?"

Houlihan was beaten down by this attack and got into a more cooperative mood. Dure shifted his mode of questioning now to a gentler, more collaborative manner. "A murderer is most likely found in one of three groups: first, family, intimate relations, and lovers; second, co-workers and business associates; and third, neighbors. So far we have no likely suspects from groups one or two, so let's look at group three."

Dure's notes at the end of the interview consisted of a list:

The Sweets – yard sign violation

The Calvattis – garbage canister violation

Loveless – illegal trapping

The Smiths – long grass violation

The Wismeres – violation of open burning regulations

The Vanderlogens – long grass violation; garbage canister violation.

* * *

A mere week remained until the start of trial. Dure had convened a brain-storming session. Dure, Kniffe, Ralph and Kara sat around the conference table in Dure's conference room. Kurt Kniffe was giving a report of his latest investigations. He spoke in a near monotone.

"The Vanderlogens left on a flight to Amsterdam on May 26 – the wife and son, that is. Mr. Vanderlogen did not fly out until two weeks later on June 9. He also flew to Amsterdam.

"Mr. Sweet says he worked late the evening of June 5, got home after dark. Didn't see anything out of the ordinary.

"Mrs. Sweet had nothing new to add to what she had told us and the police. She did comment that there was no reason for anyone to be alert to usual occurrences on Friday or Saturday, because nobody found out about the murder until Monday afternoon.

"The two Sweet girls [Kniffe pronounced this phrase without any semblance of awareness that it might have been ironic or punnable] had not been interviewed by the police. They do not recall anything about Friday. Saturday they both played field hockey. They don't remember anything worth noting the rest of the weekend. They both knew Liam Houlihan and think he is 'okay,' but his body-building over the past couple of years is 'gross.' Sometimes he visits his parents, driving a small red convertible, and he waves at them."

Kniffe looked up from the typed report he had been consulting and looked at each of his listeners in turn. No one asked him a question or said anything, so he continued.

"Loveless unfortunately was unwilling to talk to my investigator." Kniffe sounded regretful. "I therefore went to interview him myself. It was tedious. I first had an operative – well, never mind, you won't be interested in all the details – I found out the name of his homeowner's insurance company and then I went in the guise of an insurance inspector to his house. I mention this only because this particular ruse limited the type of questions I could ask him. I told him the company had learned of the crime in the neighborhood and that such occurrence might cause a rating adjustment, and that I had been sent out to assess the neighborhood. I was able to question him about the murder, and he assured me that such a thing had never happened in that development before. He said it was a domestic dispute, the husband had done it, nobody from outside was involved, and that it would seem to him on that account the neighborhood itself was not dangerous, just that particular house. He seemed quite intelligent. He had no observations of any strange vehicle or person in the neighborhood around the time of the murder. He did ask me one question, whether if someone stepped in a groundhog hole and broke their leg, would the landowner be liable?

"The last thing you asked me to check was whether one could travel between 9 Cherry Lane and 18 Locust Lane by foot under cover of wooded area. The answer is yes."

As he had been reporting, Kniffe had turned over one loose page after another in the open manila folder on the table before him, placing them face down on the left side of the open folder. Now he flipped the back of the folder over the same way, closing up the folder as if it were a book.

"With that additional information," said Dure, "let me go over the possibilities. Normally, I might look at opportunity and alibi as the first factors to limit the number of suspects. But in this case, because of the medical examiner's inability to pinpoint the time of death, almost everyone had opportunity, and almost no one an air-tight alibi. As you recall, according to the medical examiner, the time of death was between about 9:00 in the morning Friday, to about 5:00 in the afternoon on Saturday. We might be able to narrow that down based on our client's testimony that she was alive when he left the house at about 1:15, but that still makes for about 28 hours during which death could have occurred.

"If we could say that she was alive at 9:30 Friday evening, as the phone call might indicate, that would get us down to about a 20-hour time span, but that is still quite capacious, and the phone call evidence is ambiguous at best.

"So, we are forced to focus on motive." Dure did not seem happy. "And motive is tricky because what might be motive for one person would not be motive to another – like that case of the Philadelphia mobster who shot a hat-check girl through the heart because she brought him the wrong coat. To evaluate motive, then, we not only need to look at the objective facts that might give rise to tension in human relations, but also at the subjective state of mind of any particular suspect in relation to those objective facts. And, of course, we never have direct access to someone else's subjective state of mind, but can only infer what it might be based on our observations of external facts."

Here Dure allowed himself a smile which seemed to express an ironical appreciation of having outlined an insoluble problem.

Ralph had a new haircut, and he rubbed his meaty hand over the eighth-inch stubble that sparsely covered his red scalp. "If the old man didn't do it, the kid did. But the old man's admitted it. Good enough for me."

"You, Ralph," said Dure, "are why we need to find another murderer. Most jurors are going to go with the confession, and any other evidence will be ignored. The only thing that will get an acquittal is a confession of somebody else – and that not because anyone will be convinced that our client is innocent, but only because it will create reasonable doubt."

"Let's do this," said Dure. "Let's assume that everyone did it. Since we don't have a murder weapon, since we don't have a well-defined time of death, and since we don't even have a well-defined set of suspects, because the body was found out of doors – there are no fingerprints in the room, no questions of access through doors or windows – let's just assume that anyone and everyone did the crime, and then try to figure out each person's motive. The one whose motive is the most plausible should be our number one suspect."

No one objected to this manner of proceeding.

"So," said Dure. "Suppose Rhys Parker murdered Mrs. Houlihan. Why?"

Silence.

"Okay, listen," said Dure. "You don't have to believe or vouch for any motive you suggest. We just need to come up with some motive for everybody. Pretend you're writing a murder mystery novel. How would you motivate this crime?"

Kniffe said, "Suppose the strong hints we have of an affair between them are correct. Then maybe he killed her . . . out of jealousy? He wanted her to divorce her husband, he would divorce his wife, and then they would marry. But she wouldn't get a divorce, so he killed her." One could tell from the way that he said it that he did not give it much credit.

"That's a start," said Dure. "But why would he kill her because she wouldn't get a divorce?"

Kniffe shrugged. "Because that showed that she still really loved her husband and that made Parker jealous," he said.

"But do we know that they were having an affair?" asked Kara.

"It's hard to tell," said Kniffe. "One party is dead; the other is not talking. Nobody apparently caught them *in flagrante delicto*, and the third-party observations that we have are inconclusive."

"What do you think, Ralph?" said Dure.

"This the guy we saw at that model home?" said Ralph.

Dure nodded.

"Not a chance," said Ralph. "You could give that guy all the motive in the world, and he wouldn't do anything. Too much of a wimp. He's a numb-nuts."

"Thank you for that insight, Ralph," said Dure, deadpan. "Alright then, suppose Dawn Parker is the one who did it. What was her motive?"

"Obviously," said Kara, putting down her pen and looking up to address the table, "if her husband was having an affair, she could be jealous. Killing the woman would not only end the affair, it would get back at her husband."

"I don't think I mentioned that Mr. Houlihan said that he thought he saw her at the gun show," said Dure.

Kniffe made a note on the pad of paper before him.

"Anything else?" asked Dure.

No one volunteered anything. "The female of the species is deadlier than the male," quoted Dure. "How about any of the co-workers? Let's say Ms. Rittersreiter did it. What was her motive?"

"To get promoted, obviously," said Kara, after saying which she frowned dismissively and shook her head.

Dure rattled off a series of names, pausing briefly after each one to allow anyone to suggest a motive. "Chauncey Blackwell? . . . Bruno Snodhuis? . . . Nan Shuettler? . . . Megan Stoltz? . . ." A sort of silliness seemed to come over him. "Corporal Snyder? . . . Lt. Wisdom? . . . Mr. Preston? . . . Cliff Whittaker? – "

Here Kara broke in. "I vote for him. Even on the telephone he likes to take people's heads off."

Dure calmed down and smiled a wry smile. "How about Liam Houlihan?" he said. "Maybe he doesn't need a motive. Maybe he did it in a fit of so-called 'roid rage.' What do you think?"

"When people do that, get in a 'roid rage, do they remember afterwards what they did?" asked Kara. "I mean, if Liam did it, why would he let his father possibly be put to death for it – unless he maybe doesn't remember that he did it?"

"Good question, Kara. When we're done here, why don't you get me some medical articles on that question," said Dure.

"The possibility exists," said Kniffe, "that not only does Liam not know what he did, but that his father does know, and that's why he confessed, to protect his son . . . so that, if his father is convicted, it will be just what his father wanted."

"Hmm," said Dure. "One might think he'd like to get off, but maybe he figures that if he gets off, the police will re-launch their investigation and then arrest his son . . .. Hmm. Maybe that's why he sabotaged his case.

But then why did he even hire me in the first place? Why not just plead guilty and waive trial?"

"Maybe," suggested Kniffe, "he didn't know at the time he hired you that his son had done it, but found out later."

"Am I so bad a judge of character, then, that I still believe him to be innocent?" said Dure.

"He *is* innocent," returned Kniffe. "He's protecting his son."

"So you think the son did it?" said Dure.

"I did not say that," said Kniffe. "I said Houlihan thinks his son did it."

"One or the other," said Ralph. "I always said it's one or the other."

"I'm glad you have clarity on the case," said Dure to Ralph. "To me, things do not add up. I am not prepared to accept this theory. Let's move on. Let's take the case of the whole neighborhood conspiring to kill Mrs. Houlihan. Is there a plausible motive for this?"

Kniffe shook his head. "Even granting that she was the proverbial toad in the fruit salad, that's not enough for murder. Additionally, what would be the reason for a conspiracy? There is no reason why this crime could not have been done by one person acting alone."

"Are you saying this crime could not have been committed by two or more persons?" asked Dure.

"Not that it is impossible, just that there's no need for it," said Kniffe.

"Bingo!" said Ralph, slapping the table. "The old man *and* the kid did it."

Kara, sitting next to Kniffe, was doodling on a steno pad.

"Alright," said Dure, "what about the neighbors, each considered individually? The two teenage girls seem to me to be out. Agreed?"

This statement was met with a couple of shrugs and no disagreement.

"Mr. Sweet?" said Dure.

"No," said Kniffe. "The only two possibilities among the immediate neighbors are Vanderlogen and Loveless."

"Vanderlogen?" said Dure.

"Looking at just objective facts," said Kniffe, "Vanderlogen was around for two weeks after his family had gone to Holland, including the weekend of the murder, and, he has left the jurisdiction. In other words, flight. That makes him a suspect in my book."

"And the motive?" said Dure.

"He was a Dutchman," said Kniffe. "Well-known for violent tempers. You've heard of the proverbial Dutch Uncle? Mrs. Houlihan's overzealous enforcement of petty rules got under his Dutch skin."

"It would be unfortunate if he is the one who did it," said Dure. "I don't see how I can get him into court from Holland."

The telephone rang and Kara left the room to answer it.

After a pause Dure took a deep breath and said, "Contact a PI in Holland. Have him find and interview Vanderlogen. If you think he could be the one, let me know and I'll try to get the judge to pause the trial until we can --" He broke off.

Kara was standing at the door to the conference room. "It's for you," she said to Dure. "Preston."

"Enough for today," said Dure as he got up to go to his office and take the call. The session broke up.

"Hello, Walter," came Preston's voice on the telephone.

"Roderick."

"Trial is next week. We could save ourselves work by resolving the case. Suppose your guy pleads and the Commonwealth agrees not to seek the death penalty?"

"You're not offering much," said Dure.

"Just your guy's life," said Preston.

"My client is over fifty years old. Even if he gets the death sentence, there will be ten years of appeals. There's an even chance he dies before the sentence would be carried out. So the likelihood is, even if he's convicted, life in prison. What are you offering that would be worth giving up the chance for an acquittal?"

"You know as well as I do there's no chance for acquittal. Be realistic."

"As you know, I am required to discuss any offer with my client. I will do that," said Dure.

"I'll just let you know, as you and your client are discussing the matter, that I'll have a surprise for him at trial."

"Roderick, that's no use. It won't make any impression on him – or me – unless you tell me what it is."

"I like to keep some surprises."

"You'd better not be withholding Brady materials," said Dure.

"This is definitely not exculpatory," said Preston. "I'll give you a hint . . . no, actually, I won't. But you need to let me know soon. I'm only making this offer to save the Commonwealth the resources that would be expended in final trial preparation. In a couple of days I'll likely withdraw the offer."

* * *

Late Friday afternoon, a bald man wearing a lightweight, powder gray suit that was too large for him breezed in the front door of Attorney Dure's office. The suit jacket was large enough that it could have been buttoned over the protruding midsection that preceded the man, but the jacket was not buttoned, and flapped loosely at his sides. A smell of cow-manure accompanied the man as he strode to Kara's desk.

"Here you are, darling," he said to her, flopping a stack of papers on her desk and putting another paper in front of her. "Sign there," he said, pointing with a pudgy finger to a blank on the paper.

Kara looked at the paper, and instead of signing, picked up the phone and buzzed Dure. "Mr. Whittaker has some papers for you," she said into the telephone.

"All you have to do is sign acknowledgment of service," said Whittaker. "It's not a mortgage."

"Mr. Dure will be out in a minute," she said.

"Just sign it! Don't waste my time," said Whittaker.

The smell of manure was arousing Kara's curiosity and she stood up to look around, seeking its source. A set of muddy footprints ran from the front door to her desk. "Look what you've done to the carpet!" she said.

Whittaker turned to look at the carpet and laughed. "Oh! Ha, ha, ha. I was out on my farm this afternoon. Ha, ha. Lovely day."

Dure came out into the reception area. "Cliff," he said, acknowledging Whittaker's presence. "What's this about?" he asked Kara. She handed him the set of papers. He looked them over. It was a Motion to Quash Subpoena. Dure flipped through the papers. "You're representing Dawn Parker?" he asked.

"What do you think?" answered Whittaker.

"This motion's on for Monday morning," said Dure. "You're supposed to serve the motion ten days before the hearing."

"Your subpoena calls for my client's appearance on Wednesday. So I had to put in on for Monday."

"You could have filed it earlier."

"Client just retained me."

"And you serve papers Friday afternoon at 4:30?"

Whittaker shrugged. "What can I do? How about my proof of service?"

Dure nodded to Kara and she initialed Whittaker's paper and held it out to him.

He took it, gave first Kara, and then Dure, an obnoxious grin and turned to leave. At the door, he stopped, turned and looked at the carpet. He laughed. "Sue me!" he said and went out.

"Dawn Parker doesn't want to be a witness . . . Hmmm," said Dure musingly. "In addition to the other things we have to do, now we have to deal with this."

12.

We're out of time," said Dure. It was Sunday, and trial was two days off. Dure, Kara, and Ralph were in the office working on final trial preparations, as well as Whittaker's Motion to Quash.

They had interviewed Bruno Snodhuis, the political nut; Chauncey Blackwell, the big, inarticulate oaf; Ms. Rittersreiter, the librarian who was promoted into Mrs. Houlihan's position; and other people. Dure or Kniffe had interviewed all of the neighbors except for Mr. Vanderlogen, who was still out of the country. Nothing. They had interviewed Mrs. Houlihan's co-workers, although some would not talk. Results from all of this: nothing.

They had no one they could point to, other than the possibility of suggesting by innuendo that Liam Houlihan had done it, but then Mr. Houlihan forbad even that. In response to Dure's request for Brady materials, Preston had sent useless junk. So, Dure had nothing, and the trial was to begin. Preston, apparently believing that he had an open and shut case, had withdrawn his plea offer.

The long and the short of it was, that there was no clear and definite proof that anyone had killed Mrs. Houlihan – except, that is, for Dure's client, who admitted doing it.

Mr. Houlihan would not be convinced that the death penalty was a realistic possibility, and he frankly said, even if it is, I don't care. I'm old anyway.

Dure told his team that because of Mr. Houlihan's confession, it would not be sufficient to throw off sparks of suspicion in all directions in hopes of creating reasonable doubt. They would not get an acquittal unless they could show that somebody else had committed the murder.

The best remaining chance would be to get the real murderer on the stand and provoke some self-incriminating statement. For this reason, Dure, after looking at the witness list which the prosecution had served on him, had served subpoenas on Snodhuis and Blackwell; both Parkers were already under subpoena. And Dawn Parker had hired a lawyer to try to quash her subpoena. Hmm.

* * *

The next morning at the hearing on Attorney Whittaker's Motion to Quash, Whittaker tried to put Dure in a box: either explain why the defense needed Dawn Parker as a witness, or give up the subpoena. Dure did not want to give away information that would alert Parker to either his trial strategy or his reason for wanting her at trial. So Dure only explained his need for the witness in vague generalities: background information about the victim, and in a capital case, the defense should be given full latitude to defend without having to disclose its trial strategy.

Fortunately for Dure, Judge Ozma, the young woman with the lime green fingernails, was impatient that morning and denied Whittaker's motion without, seemingly, giving much attention to either lawyer's argument.

"I'll renew the motion before the trial judge," snarled Whittaker as he and Dure walked out of the courtroom.

Thus were two hours of Dure's time wasted on the day before trial.

* * *

"Ladies and gentlemen of the jury," began Mr. Preston in his opening statement, "this is a simple case of extreme domestic violence. Medical evidence will show that Mrs. Tiffany Houlihan died a brutal death. You will see photographs of her decapitated body as it was found in the backyard of the marital home.

"The Commonwealth will show, by testimony of neighbors, that there had been long-standing domestic strife between Mr. Houlihan and his wife.

"Experienced police homicide detectives will testify that Mr. Houlihan called the police late Monday morning to report a dead body in his yard. When the police responded to the site, they found the body of Mrs. Houlihan in the condition which you will see in photographs. The detectives then interviewed Mr. Houlihan, who said that he had left home the preceding Friday at approximately 1:15 in the afternoon and did not return home until Monday morning, when he called the police. Mr. Houlihan, at that time, also denied having anything to do with the death of his wife.

"Testimony of medical experts will establish the probable time of death as being from Friday morning to early Friday afternoon – a time frame during which Mr. Houlihan admittedly was at home.

"Police detectives will testify that from the beginning, their interest centered on Mr. Houlihan, and that in the course of their investigation they did not find any suspects with motive or opportunity other than Mr. Houlihan. The detectives will tell you, from the witness stand, that after ten days of investigation, they re-interviewed Mr. Houlihan, at which time . . . *he broke down and confessed to killing his wife*." Preston paused here to let that sink in. "At the request of the detectives, Mr. Houlihan signed a written statement confessing to the murder. The Commonwealth will introduce into evidence a video recording of the confession and the original document signed by Mr. Houlihan, and you will be able to examine it in the jury room.

"At the conclusion of the presentation of all the evidence, ladies and gentlemen, the Commonwealth believes that you will be convinced, beyond any reasonable doubt, that Mr. Howard Houlihan, the man sitting at the defense table, right over there, did willfully and with malice aforethought, kill and murder his wife, and that you will return a verdict of *Guilty*.

"Ladies and gentlemen of the jury, thank you for your attention."

"Ladies and gentlemen of the jury," said Dure, looking remarkably handsome in a freshly pressed suit, but still with his habitual glum expression, "If there were a genuine, good-faith confession in this case, then why have the police not recovered the murder weapon? And why have they not recovered the head? The defense is not going to dispute that the poor woman was murdered. But the question at issue will be: who did it? *Who* did it?

"Are you going to believe that someone would confess to a murder, and then, as if it were some kind of game, some crazy version of hide-and-seek, refuse to disclose what he did with the murder weapon, and where he disposed of part of the body?

"Ladies and gentlemen, watch for what the prosecution does not tell you. There will be no eyewitness to the killing. There will be no fingerprints of Mr. Houlihan on any instrumentality of death. There will be no murder weapon introduced into evidence. There will be no evidence of the whereabouts of the poor woman's head.

"When you have seen all the evidence, ladies and gentlemen, you will be left wondering what happened. It will be a far cry from proof beyond a reasonable doubt.

"Ladies and gentlemen, I thank you for your kind attention, and I invite your closest attention to the trial that is to follow. For a man's life is at stake. Mr. Houlihan could have plea-bargained, but instead, trusting in his innocence, he gives his fate to the judgment of a jury –"

"Objection!" said Mr. Preston. "Highly improper for the defense to mention plea negotiations."

"Your honor," said Dure, "I mentioned no negotiations, but merely said that Mr. Houlihan did not choose to plea bargain."

"Mr. Dure," said the judge, "you were just about to conclude your opening?"

"I was, Your Honor."

"You have just a sentence or two?"

"Half a sentence, Your Honor,"

"Alright, you finish and let's move this case along."

"Thank you, Your Honor," said Dure

"Ladies and gentlemen, as I was saying, Mr. Houlihan is trusting his fate to the fair and impartial judgment of a jury of his peers. Thank you."

Live-blogging from the court in the Houlihan trial. [post] *Opening statements just completed. The defense opening statement was well delivered, but short on substance. Either the defense doesn't have much, or defense attorney Dure is holding back for tactical reasons.* [post] Torvald Bornstein's head was bowed down as he concentrated on his typing. He did not notice the bailiff go up to the side of the bench and claim the judge's attention.

After talking with the bailiff, the judge scooted his chair over to the center of the bench. "I have been informed that someone in the courtroom is using an electronic device." The judge looked at the bailiff, who had gone to the barrier separating the well of the court from the spectator seating, and was pointing directly at Bornstein.

"Stand up, Sir," said the judge.

"Who, me?" said Bornstein, looking up suddenly, startled.

"You," said the judge. "What are you doing?"

Bornstein seemed to know that he had been caught and seemed desperate for an answer. "What am I doing?" he asked.

"That's right, what are you doing?" said the judge, in a deadpan, ironic tone of voice. He too seemed to know that Bornstein had been caught, and because of Bornstein's evasiveness, was going to enjoy his unmasking.

"I'm . . . I'm just typing."

"And what are you typing on?" asked the judge.

Bornstein held up his i-pad.

"Is that an electronic device capable of transmitting outside of this courtroom?" asked the judge. Without waiting for an answer, he said, "Bailiff, bring that device to the bench."

As the bailiff was moving to carry out the judge's instructions, Bornstein said, "Yes, sir."

"My Standing Order is very clear that electronic devices capable of transmission are not permitted in jury trials. That means Blackberries, smart phones . . . and i-pads."

The bailiff carried the i-pad to the bench. The judge looked at the i-pad. "You are making public commentary on the trial?" he asked Bornstein.

"Yes, sir."

"And transmitting your commentary presumably to some blog or news site or something similar?"

"To the Coke's Law Blog," said Bornstein.

"I appreciate your candor," said the judge. "Because of that, I am only going to sentence you to twenty-four hours in jail. I had thought of five days. I find you in contempt of court for violating the Standing Order of this Court. Let the record show that the contempt occurred in open court. The Court will also confiscate the electronic device which was used in the contempt. The sentence will start immediately. Bailiff, take the gentleman into custody."

The courtroom was silent while Bornstein was removed by the bailiff.

"Proceed, Mr. Preston," said the judge, when Bornstein was gone.

The prosecution called Cleveland McCann, M.D., medical examiner. Dr. McCann testified that based on his examination of the corpse that the woman was dead, that she had been decapitated, that she had not committed suicide, that the probable time of death was from Friday morning to early Friday afternoon, that this determination was based on the contents of the deceased's stomach, that she appeared to have eaten something fatty that would take some time to digest, that it probably was cheese, and that the deceased had probably consumed it at lunch time.

"No further question," said Preston.

Dure was whispering to his client. "One of the things I want to do," he said, "is emphasize to the point of ridiculousness that the prosecution has not located the head."

"Counselor?" said the judge.

Dure stood to cross-examine. "Doctor, you did not examine a corpse, did you?"

"Of course I did."

"Isn't it true that you examined a body part without a head?

"I examined a corpse without a head."

"Well, a body without a head is not a corpse, isn't that right?"

"You can call it a corpse."

"Well, you can call a Buick a hot air balloon, can't you?"

"I suppose."

"You suppose? Isn't it true that you can call a Buick a hot air balloon?"

"Yes."

"But a Buick is not a hot air balloon, isn't that right?"

"Yes."

"So, I repeat, you did not examine a corpse, did you?"

"I repeat, I did."

"Is a head important?"

"Is a head important? Yes, a head is important."

"A corpse is a dead human being?"

"Yes."

"And a human being is not complete without a head, isn't that right?"

"I suppose."

"You suppose? Would you consider yourself a human being if you didn't have a head?"

"Counselor!" said the judge.

"It's cross-examination, Your Honor," said Dure.

"Come to the point, counselor," admonished the judge.

Dure turned again to the witness. "This thing which you examined, and which you want to call a corpse, did not have a head?"

"No."

"That being so, you did not examine the teeth of this body part, did you?"

"No."

"And that being so, no check of dental records could be made for purposes of identification, isn't that so?"

"Yes."

"So you have no idea of the identity of the person to whom this body part belonged?"

"Identifying the deceased was not part of my duties."

"Would you please answer my question: you have no idea of the identity of the person to whom this body part belonged?"

"I did not identify the corpse, no."

"You did not note the existence of any tattoos on the body part that you examined?"

"I don't recall noting any, no."

"In fact, you did not record in your report any peculiar identifying characteristics on the body part which you examined?"

"The corpse was in a state of partial decomposition."

"Would you please answer my question: you did not record in your report any peculiar identifying characteristics on the body part which you examined?"

"I don't recall."

"Would you like to review your report to refresh your memory?"

"Thank you."

Dure went to the defense table and retrieved a copy of the doctor's report. "Your Honor, may I approach the witness?"

"You may," said the judge.

Dure gave the report to the doctor, then said, "Take your time, doctor."

"No, I don't see any."

"So, based on your examination, doctor, there is no way that the identity of the deceased could be determined?"

"Not on my report, no. But again, identifying the deceased was not part of my duties."

"Thank you, doctor. Now doctor, you gave as your opinion that the cause of death was decapitation, isn't that so?"

"Yes."

"But isn't it possible that the corpse lost its head after the person was dead?"

"I suppose so."

"You do a lot of supposing, doctor. Isn't it possible that the corpse lost its head after the person was dead, yes or no?"

"That is medically possible, yes."

"Medically possible. It is also non-medically possible, isn't that right?"

"I don't know what you mean by "non-medically." My job is to render a medical opinion."

"The point is, a head can be cut off a corpse, whether by a doctor or a butcher, or anybody else?"

"Yes."

"And in point of fact, wouldn't it be easier to cut the head off a corpse than off a living person?"

"I suppose so."

"You suppose so. Don't you know, or is that beyond your medical expertise?"

"It seems reasonable. I haven't tried it myself."

There was laughter in the courtroom.

"You examined the body part for signs of struggle, did you not?"

"I examined the corpse for scratches, bruises, foreign matter, things that would indicate struggle or resistance, yes."

"And you found none, isn't that right?"

"You have to remember that the corpse was in a state of partial decomposition."

"Doctor, would you please answer my question: you found no signs of struggle, did you?"

"No."

"Doctor, in your medical opinion, wouldn't the fact of absence of signs of struggle indicate that the deceased was already dead when the head was removed?"

"I can't answer that on account of the decomposition which had taken place. There might have been signs of struggle which were lost."

"Doctor, you did toxicological tests?"

"I did not, but I understand that they were done."

"And the results were made available to you?"

"Yes."

"And did you take those results into account when rendering your opinion about the cause of death?"

"Yes."

"And those tests were for commonly abused substances?"

"Basically, yes."

"A test was done for the presence of alcohol?"

"Yes, but you have to consider the time factor. Alcohol may have been metabolized, or may have evaporated."

"No alcohol was found?"

"No."

"A test was done for marijuana?

"For cannabis, yes."

"For methamphetamines?'"

"Yes. And their metabolites."

"And all of these tests returned negative results?"

"Yes."

"Was a test done for arsenic?"

"Not to my knowledge."

"Was a test done for any substance commonly used as a poison."

"It is not possible to test for everything."

"So the answer is, no tests were done for substances commonly used as poisons?"

"Not to my knowledge."

"So, doctor, it would be possible, that the deceased was poisoned, and thereafter, the head was taken off, isn't that right?"

"I-I, I couldn't say."

"Come now, doctor, the woman could have been poisoned, and after she was dead, her head could have been removed, isn't that right?"

"That would be speculation."

"You're right. That would be speculation. And I am asking you if that speculation is admissible from a medical point of view?"

"I couldn't say."

"In fact, doctor, the deceased could have died from any number of causes, and after death, the head removed?"

"I'm not willing to speculate."

"In fact, your opinion that the deceased died from decapitation is speculation?"

"Whatever else may have occurred, the body was decapitated, which would be a sufficient cause of death."

"You've admitted that no tests were done to determine whether the deceased was poisoned."

"Not that I know of."

"So, the deceased could have died from poisoning?"

"I suppose."

"She could have died from a gunshot wound to the head?"

"I suppose."

"She could have died from a knife wound cutting the carotid artery?"

"Possibly."

"The fact is, she could have died from any number of causes, and you don't have a clue as to what the real cause of death might have been?"

The doctor did not answer.

"Doctor? Did you hear the question?"

"No."

"Should I repeat it?"

"No, I mean, I heard the question . . . I don't know."

Here Dure stopped questioning and went to the defense table and stood still, staring at his papers. The courtroom was quiet. He shuffled among his papers for several moments. Then with papers in hand, he returned to the podium. With more questions, he got the doctor to admit that contrary to his written opinion, the time of death could have occurred anytime between Friday morning and Saturday afternoon; and that it was difficult to tell on account of the decomposition of the body. It was just after one o'clock and the judge declared recess for lunch.

When the court reconvened, the prosecution called Elfina Thistle to the stand. She testified that she lived one street over from the Houlihans. One Saturday, mid-morning, she had been walking her dog and passed by the Houlihans' house. She heard "extremely loud" screaming coming from the backyard of the Houlihans' house. She stood there for a few moments because her dog was marking his territory, and she heard, "You don't tell me what to do! Who are you? How do you have the nerve to even take up space? Useless!" It was a woman's voice, shrill, so high-pitched, and under such pressure, that it almost cracked.

Dure rose to cross-examine. "Mrs. Thistle, this incident you related took place some time ago?"

"About . . . nine years."

"About nine years ago?"

"Yes."

"It could have been ten?"

"Maybe. I don't think so."

"At any rate, you are not one hundred percent sure exactly when this took place?"

"No, not one hundred percent."

"You did not see anybody?"

"No."

"You did not see the person who was shouting?"

"No."

"You did not see anyone else?"

"No."

"So you do not know if more than one person was present?"

"Well, she had to be talking to someone?"

"That is your assumption?"

"Well, of course."

"And if we go along with your assumption, you did not see to whom this woman was talking?"

"No."

"It could have been a dog?"

"It didn't sound like it – and I don't think the Houlihans had a dog."

"But you did not see who it was?"

"No. "

"It could have been anybody?"

"I mean, who would it be? Saturday morning, in the backyard?"

"That is my point. You did not see, and you do not know?"

"That is true."

"No further questions."

The judge said, "I see that it is ten minutes before five. Court will stand adjourned until ten o'clock tomorrow morning."

The next morning, as the various actors filtered into court, Prosecutor Preston seemed to be intentionally keeping a poker face; but it was unmistakable that there was a certain buzz going on in the prosecution team.

When the judge called the court to order, Preston called Lieutenant Harold Wisdom to the witness box. He first established that Lt. Wisdom was a member of the Canterbury police force, and that he had investigated this case and was familiar with it. "Lt. Wisdom, have you recently done further investigation in this case?"

"Yes."

"What were you looking for, and what did you find?"

"As you know, the defense has been complaining that the victim's head has not been located."

"Yes, we're all aware of that."

"Right. And it's something we have been searching for all along. When the defense raised the question in court yesterday, I went back to the file and looked through it carefully. Then I had some officers re-search the residence, the grounds around it, and the defendant's shave-ice trailer."

"Did you find anything?"

"Yes, sir. We found the missing head."

Mild gasps could be heard in the courtroom.

"Where did you find it?

"In the defendant's shave-ice trailer."

Exclamations sounded in the courtroom.

"There will be order!" said the judge.

Mr. Preston continued. "Where in the defendant's shave-ice trailer?"

"In the back of the trailer, the part where the shave-ice was prepared, there is a refrigeration unit. We found it in there."

"I show you this photograph of the inside of the back of the defendant's shave ice trailer. Is this an accurate depiction of what it shows?"

"Yes."

Preston addressed the judge. "Your Honor, the Commonwealth moves the admission of this photograph in evidence. Commonwealth's Exhibit No. 5."

Preston gave the photograph to Dure to inspect. He, in turn, showed it to his client.

Sounding disgusted, Dure said, "No objection."

"The photograph is admitted," said the judge.

Preston placed the photograph on the projection device, which caused the image to be displayed on the computer screens throughout the courtroom.

"Now Lieutenant," said Preston, "may I ask you to step down from the stand and, using this marker, indicate exactly where the head was found?"

The Lieutenant drew a circle on the photograph around a stainless steel refrigeration unit. When the Lieutenant returned to the stand, Preston continued: "Now, Lieutenant, I show you *this* photograph. Will you tell the court what it shows?"

"That's the head. That's what we discovered in the refrigeration unit."

The same procedure of admitting the photograph into evidence was performed.

"May it please the Court," said Preston, "since this photograph is rather gruesome, I request the Court's permission to show it to the jury by passing it from juror to juror, rather than to put it up on the display."

"Mr. Dure?" said the judge.

"No objection," said Dure.

"Alright, Mr. Preston," said the judge. "You may show the photograph to the jury."

Preston took the photograph and handed it to juror number one. This was a man in his fifties with a mustache. His face expressed revulsion, and he passed the photograph to the next juror, a stiff-looking woman in an olive-colored dress. She took one glance, quickly turned her head away and passed the photograph on. When all fourteen jurors had seen the photograph, Preston re-took possession of it.

"No further questions, Your Honor," said Preston.

Dure stood up to cross-examine.

"Lieutenant, where was this trailer when you found this . . . evidence in it?"

"In the garage of the defendant's house."

"Did you have a search warrant to enter the premises?"

"We did."

"Did you have a search warrant to enter the trailer."

"We did."

"Does the Canterbury police force do slip-shod work?"

"No."

"Would you say the Canterbury police force is a professional force?"

"Yes."

"The Canterbury police force performs its work professionally?"

"Yes."

"Especially on a murder case, is the Canterbury police force is careful in its work?"

"We are careful in all of our work."

"Then, you don't make any special effort to be thorough in the investigation of a murder?"

"I'm not sure what you mean by 'special effort.'"

"An effort more meticulous than, say, in a case of a stolen bicycle?"

"We obviously deploy more resources in investigating a murder than a stolen bicycle. Murder is the most serious crime. We deal with it with the seriousness it deserves."

"In a murder investigation, is the Canterbury police for thorough and complete in its work?"

"Objection," said Preston. "Counsel is badgering the witness."

"Your Honor," said Dure, "this is cross-examination in a murder trial. The prosecution gave no notice of this evidence – it's an ambush witness – and then the prosecutor runs interference for the witness on cross-examination. I am wondering what is the Commonwealth afraid of."

"Your Honor," said Preston. "We just discovered this evidence yesterday evening. This is the earliest we could have given notice."

"Gentlemen," said the judge. "approach the bench."

When the lawyers and the court reporter had gathered at the far corner of the bench, the judge said, "I do not like this kind of argument and speaking motion in front of the jury. If you have anything more than a one- or two-word objection, approach the bench with it. Don't toy with me on this. I can hold either or both of you in contempt. You are on notice. As to this particular objection, I will overrule the objection."

The players returned to their places.

"Now," said Dure. "You – and by you, I mean the Canterbury police force – searched this trailer on Monday, June 8, when you first investigated this crime, isn't that correct?"

"Yes."

"And you searched it thoroughly?"

"I would assume so. Again, I did not personally conduct that search."

"Wouldn't you agree, Lieutenant, that the fact that the police searched the trailer on June 8 without finding this head is conclusive evidence that the head was not in the trailer on June 8?"

The lieutenant's face was becoming flushed. "Not conclusive," he said. "Unfortunately, sometimes people make mistakes."

"Not only did the police search the trailer on June 8, but they searched it so thoroughly that they released the trailer back to the defendant at the end of the day, isn't that right?"

"Yes." The lieutenant was curt.

"Now, wouldn't you conclude that the head that you found last night had been placed in the trailer after June 8?"

"That is certainly a possibility."

"What efforts have the police made to determine how and when and by whom the head was placed in the trailer?"

"We just found it last night."

"In other words, the police have made no efforts to determine how and when and by whom the head was placed in the trailer?"

"I don't think that's correct. We do not have any reportable results in such a short time."

"What specific efforts have the police made to determine how and when and by whom the head was placed in the trailer?"

"I don't know."

"You will agree with me that the defendant could not have done it while he was in custody?"

"That makes sense."

"Is it true or not true that the that the defendant could not have placed that head in his trailer while he was being held in custody?"

The lieutenant looked over at Houlihan. Houlihan was wearing the same pained expression he had been wearing for most of the trial. There was now, however, an added note of curiosity in his face. The lieutenant said, "I do not see how he could have, but I am not going to say that it was impossible."

"You are not willing to say that it was impossible. So, you are saying that it *was* possible for the defendant to have escaped from jail, gone somewhere to retrieve the head, gone to his home, planted it in his own trailer, then, got back into jail, all without being discovered?"

The lieutenant's face turned red again. "No, that would not have been possible."

"Thank you, Lieutenant. Now, I noticed that the photograph produced by the prosecution was of the exterior of the refrigeration unit. Did the police take any photographs of the inside of that unit?"

"I believe so."

"Did you give copies or originals of those photographs to the prosecution?"

"I would have to think that we did."

"Your Honor," said Dure. "I should like for the prosecution to produce those photographs."

"Mr. Preston?" said the judge.

"We will produce them, Your Honor."

"When might we expect them?" asked Dure.

"We will do it by close of business today, Your Honor," said Preston.

"No further questions," said Dure.

"I have some re-direct," said Preston.

"Proceed," said the judge.

"Lieutenant, when was the defendant arrested?"

The lieutenant checked his file again, "It was early in the morning of June 16."

"And when did the police release the trailer into the possession of the defendant?"

"On the afternoon – or evening – of June 8."

"So, the defendant could have put the head in his own trailer during that week from June 8 to June 15?"

"Yes, he could have."

"Now, Lieutenant, I am sure that defense counsel would love to argue that there would be no reason for the defendant to do such a thing. In your professional experience as a law enforcement officer, can you suggest why a murderer in the defendant's position might have done such a thing?"

"Objection," said Dure. "Calls for speculation."

"Approach the bench," said the judge.

At the bench conference, the judge said, "I told you, Mr. Dure, no more than one or two words in an objection. You are skating on thin ice. I do not like lawyers to put argument to the jury through the form of objections."

"I apologize, Your Honor," said Dure. "The point seemed so obvious that I merely said it automatically."

"Mr. Preston?" said the judge.

"Your Honor, the lieutenant is obviously an expert in law enforcement, and as an expert, he is permitted to opine on hypothetical questions. It is equally obvious what argument defense counsel wants to make, and the Commonwealth is entitled to put in evidence to counter it."

"If it please the Court --" said Dure.

"The objection is overruled," said the judge, cutting off Dure's argument. The bench conference was over.

Preston now re-asked the question.

"For one thing," answered the lieutenant, "in my experience, criminals often do stupid things. Sometimes you just have to scratch your head trying to understand their actions. But, in this case, a clever criminal might have reasoned that, because the police had already searched his trailer, it would be a good hiding place. He would anticipate that we would not search it again. And we wouldn't have, if the defense hadn't made such a big deal in court yesterday about the head's not being found."

"Thank you, lieutenant. You've been very helpful." Preston let the jury see his big smile.

"Do you wish to re-cross-examine the witness?" said the judge to Dure.

"Your Honor, I should like to defer re-cross until we receive the photographs promised by the prosecution."

"Very well," said the judge.

"The Commonwealth re-calls Dr. Cleveland McCann as its next witness," said Preston.

When Dr. McCann had taken the witness stand, Preston began with: "Dr. McCann, you had earlier examined the corpse identified as belonging to Tiffany Houlihan, did you not?"

"Indeed, yes, as I earlier testified."

"Now, last night you were asked to do further examination, were you not?"

"Late last night, yes," said the doctor, seeming put out about it.

"Please tell the Court about that examination," said Preston.

"I was presented with a desiccated caput," testified the doctor. "I found a penetrating wound in the dextral tempora. Upon performing an exploratory section, I found and extracted a lead pellet. This pellet, or bullet you might call it, had penetrated the frontal lobe to the corpus callosum and was undoubtedly the cause of near-instantaneous death. An unusual phenomenon with this specimen is that the laceration of the epidermis had been cauterized, as had the wall of the penetration wound."

"Doctor, when you mentioned the bullet had penetrated the frontal lobe, you meant the brain, right?"

"Yes, in layman's terms, the brain."

"And for my benefit, what does 'cauterize' mean?"

"That means singed, or burned."

Preston retrieved a small plastic baggie from the prosecution's table. "I show you this bullet and ask if you can identify it."

The doctor took the baggie in his hand and peered at what was in it. "Yes, this is the pellet which I removed from the caput."

"Doctor, were you able to identify to whom this head belonged?"

Dure leaned over to whisper to Houlihan. While Dure and Houlihan were whispering, something the doctor said grabbed Dure's attention. Dure sat upright and turned to give his attention to the testimony. The doctor was saying, "The blood type, AB negative, is consistent with the blood type of the body previously identified as Tiffany Houlihan . . . and this morning I received a report from a forensic orthodontologist stating that the caput is that of Tiffany Houlihan."

"Thank you, Doctor, no further questions."

"Is the Commonwealth not going to move the introduction of the bullet in evidence?" asked Dure.

Preston, having already sat down, stood again and addressed the judge: "No, Your Honor."

"May I see it?" asked Dure.

Preston delivered the baggie to Dure, who looked closely at it, then opened the baggie and poured the bullet out. He approached the witness. "Doctor, this bullet seems to be strangely deformed. Is this the condition in which you recovered it from the head?"

"Yes."

"You did not do anything to it to deform it or modify it?"

"I did nothing to it, not even clean it. It was exactly in that shape when I removed it from the caput."

"If I may," said Preston, standing and interrupting, "the Commonwealth can present testimony to establish a chain of custody, and I will represent to the Court that that is the bullet that was removed from the head."

"I will accept that," said Dure, "and the defense moves the admission of this bullet in evidence."

"Does the prosecution object?" said the judge.

Preston looked annoyed, but he said, "No objection."

"It will be admitted as exhibit D-1," said the judge.

"Doctor," said Dure, "you previously opined that the cause of death was decapitation. Does this evidence change your opinion?"

"Well . . . not really. Decapitation remains a sufficient cause of death."

"Doctor, I suggest to you that the victim had been shot in the head and thereafter was decapitated. Is that within the realm of medical possibility?"

"It's possible, yes."

Dure nodded. The doctor volunteered a clarifying comment. "We have no way of knowing if the decedent had been shot first or decapitated first."

"You think maybe somebody cut off the head and then used it for target practice?" asked Dure with such pronounced sarcasm that the doctor's face flushed.

"Well, the other thing is," said the doctor, trying to recover, "even if the decedent had been shot, we have no way of knowing if death had occurred before the decapitation."

"I see," said Dure. "How deep was the bullet buried in the brain?"

"It was, if I recall correctly, about five inches," said the doctor.

"And it's your medical opinion that a person could survive that?"

"Well, not long, but maybe long enough that the decapitation was in fact the efficient cause of death."

"Just a few minutes ago you testified that it caused near-instantaneous death."

"Well, there's a certain range of variation and uncertainty in these things."

"Doctor, did you examine the skin around the bullet entry for powder burns?"

"I did, and found none."

"Indicating that the head was some distance away from the muzzle of the weapon that fired the bullet?"

"I'm not a firearms expert. I'll just say that no powder residue was found on the caput."

"No further questions," said Dure.

13.

"M r. Dure!" called Torvald Bornstein, as Dure was approaching the entrance to the Justice Center the next morning. Dure stopped and returned the contumacious blogger's greeting.

"Can you fill me in on what happened yesterday?" asked Bornstein, puffing a bit from the exertion of walking hurriedly.

"Are you still going to blog this case?" asked Dure.

Bornstein smiled sheepishly. His head swayed in indecision. "I've paid enough for the privilege," he said. "I could go in and take notes by hand and then post them from outside the courtroom during breaks. I'm still deciding what to do. But from the comments and traffic on my site, there is interest in this case."

Seeming to take pity on the man, Dure gave him a rather detailed commentary. Bornstein took out a small notebook and scribbled rapidly. "You have any hope you're going to get an acquittal?" he asked.

The question elicited from Dure a sardonic grimace; but he answered with an air of patience. "From yesterday's testimony and evidence, I am pretty sure I now know how the murder was done. If I am right, then I also have a pretty good idea of who did it. But don't print that. I don't want to scare somebody off. I'll be attempting to confirm my hypothesis today."

"Oh, come on, come on. You gotta tell me more than that."

"Come into court and watch," said Dure.

"Yeahh . . . I'm not so sure . . . " said Bornstein.

Dure joined the flow of persons entering the Complex.

* * *

As soon as the judge had taken his seat, Preston announced, "The Commonwealth calls Everett Loveless as its next witness."

Interrupting, Dure said, "If I may, Your Honor, the defense would like to finish its cross examination of Lt. Wisdom, now that we have the photographs the prosecution promised."

"Yes, I recall," said the judge. "Lt. Wisdom to the stand."

Preston frowned and sat down.

"May I approach the witness?" said Dure, holding a photograph in his hand.

"You may," said the judge.

"Lt. Wisdom, this is a photograph which the police took of the interior of the refrigeration unit where the head was found, is it not?"

"Yes."

"And directing your attention to the bottom of the inside of the unit, would you agree with me that there is no accumulation of blood or other fluid there?"

"Yes, that's right. There was no blood."

"Which would indicate that the head had been placed there some considerable time after it had been severed?"

"It could indicate that."

"Thank you, Lieutenant," said Dure. He walked to the defense table and put down the photograph, then went to the clerk's bench and took up the baggie with the bullet in it. He glanced at the judge to see whether he needed to ask permission again to approach the witness, but the judge nodded, and Dure proceeded to the witness stand.

"Lt. Wisdom, I show you this bullet which has been removed from the head which your department recovered. You have examined and are familiar with this?"

"I have examined it, yes."

"Would you agree that this is probably a .22 caliber bullet?"

"It certainly could be. But as you will note, the bullet is deformed. Could be a .25 caliber."

"Did you weigh the bullet?"

"We did."

"And what was the weight?"

"Thirty-nine grains."

"And the standard weight for the most common .22 Long Rifle ammunition is 40 grains?"

"That's right."

"And nearly all .25 caliber ammunition carries a bullet significantly heavier than 40 grains?"

"Generally, yes."

"Thank you, Lieutenant. No further questions."

Now Preston called Everett Loveless to the stand. "This will be the prosecution's last witness," said Preston to the judge.

Loveless testified that he had lived next door to the Houlihans for the past 15 years. He was familiar with the Houlihan family.

"Do you recognize Mr. Houlihan here in the courtroom?"

"Of course."

"Would you point him out for the jury?"

Loveless pointed with his entire arm and forefinger extended at Houlihan.

Then Preston took Loveless through a series of questions in which Loveless, reluctantly, told of observing violent arguments between Houlihan and his wife. According to what Preston was able to drag out of Loveless, these had occurred, at least to his observation, at long intervals over the whole course of the time that they had been neighbors. About two years ago he had overheard an especially loud, violent argument coming from the Houlihans' back yard. He had heard a sharp smack that sounded like it could have been a slap, but he could not say, assuming it was a slap, who had slapped whom. Since then, he had not heard any arguments, but he had noticed that Mr. Houlihan had become less outgoing, and seemed beaten down. Even his posture had suffered.

As to the weekend of the murder, he had not noticed anything unusual. He had seen Houlihan drive away on Friday afternoon, but was uncertain what time that had been. He had been out in his front yard. The next thing he knew about what was going on next door was Monday when police cars started arriving. He had been as shocked as anyone else in the neighborhood. On that note, Preston relinquished the witness to Dure.

Dure stood. "Your Honor, if I may. I would like to call a witness to lay a foundation before I begin my cross-examination of this witness."

"I object," said Preston. "The defense can call its witnesses during its own case. This is the prosecution's case."

"Your Honor," said Dure. "The laying of the foundation will not take long – no more than five minutes. Without it, I cannot do a proper cross . . . and the defense does not intend to call Mr. Loveless as a witness in the defense case."

"If it will only take five minutes," said the judge, "I'll allow it. Go ahead."

"I call Manolete Gonzalez," said Dure.

Loveless vacated the witness chair and a barrel-chested Hispanic man of about 40 came forward. Mr. Gonzalez testified that he was the crew chief for the crew that mowed the lawn of the Sweets, across the street from Mr. Loveless's residence. He stated that the company he worked for had a contract with the Sweets for weekly mowing, and that unless weather conditions interfered, they mowed the lawn on Fridays, usually about mid-day, it being the third house on his Friday route. According to company records and his memory, they had mowed that lawn starting around 12:30 on Friday the 5th of June, and that it usually took about an hour. Then Dure asked:

"What kind of mower did you use?"

"It was a TurfChomper 66-inch 31-horsepower, Front Mount, Zero Turn Mower," said Gonzalez.

"Do you wear hearing protection while using that mower?"

"Oh, yes sir. Those mowers are very loud."

"The manual that comes with those mowers requires hearing protection, does it not?"

"Yes, sir, it does."

"And, at my request, did you check the manual for a decibel rating on that mower?"

"Yes, sir. It is between 95 and 100 decibels according to the manual."

"And you brought the manual with you?"

"Yes sir, I have it right here."

"Thank you. I don't need to look at it, but maybe the prosecution will want to."

"And while you are operating the mower, is any other noise-producing equipment being used?"

"Objection," called out Preston. "This whole line of questions is irrelevant."

Dure started to respond to the objection, but the judge held up his hand to Dure to be quiet. Then the judge said, "I think, since the witness has testified that this was occurring during the time which the prosecution maintains that the crime was committed, I will allow it."

"While I am running the big mower," said Gonzalez, "another man is using a trimmer or a blower."

"And how loud, in decibels are these?"

"They are very loud. As you said, I look in the manuals and they up to 110 decibels."

"Thank you, Mr. Gonzalez. No further questions."

"Do you wish to cross-examine?" asked the judge of Preston.

"No, Your Honor, I do not wish to further waste the Court's time."

Mr. Gonzales left the witness stand, and Mr. Loveless returned to it. Dure begin his cross-examination. "Mr. Loveless, continuing to direct your attention to the weekend of the murder, on Friday, June 5, you did not notice anything unusual in the Houlihans' yard?"

"No-o." Loveless made the word almost two syllables, drawing it out into a wary question.

"You did not notice any strange vehicles in the neighborhood?"

"No."

"You did not notice any strange persons in the neighborhood?"

"No."

"You did not notice any unusual activity in or around the Houlihans' yard?"

"No."

Dure asked exactly the same set of four questions with respect to Saturday, June 6. He got a 'no' to each question. Then he asked exactly the same set of questions for Sunday, June 7, and got a 'no' to each of those questions as well. Then he asked the same set of four questions again about Monday, June 8 up until the time that the first police car arrived on the scene. He got a 'no' in response to each question.

Then he shifted gears. "It's true, isn't it, that in your neighborhood there is a lot of road kill?" he asked.

Loveless appeared startled for a moment. "I don't know about 'a lot,'" he said.

"You've seen flattened squirrels on the roads around your house?"

"Yes."

"'Possums?"

"Yes."

"The occasional raccoon?"

"Yes."

"Deer?"

"Yes."

Preston got to his feet. "I object, Your Honor. May we approach the bench?"

"Come forward," said the judge.

The two attorneys advanced to the side of the bench that was away from the jury, and the court reporter nimbly lifted and carried his transcribing machine to join them.

"I let Mr. Dure go for a while," said Preston, "in part because I couldn't believe my ears. But his questions are not only absurd, they have nothing whatever to do with the case. He's wasting the time of the Court and the jury."

The judge turned to Dure and lifted his eyebrows by way of asking for Dure's response.

"This is a murder case, Your Honor – " said Dure.

Preston interrupted. "Exactly, Your Honor. It has nothing to do with vehicular manslaughter of local fauna."

"Let him talk," said the judge.

"It is well established," continued Dure, "that defense counsel in cross-examination should be allowed the widest latitude. The defendant's life is at stake and I am entitled to cross-examine in the way I see fit to best defend my client."

"Can you tell the Court in what way this line of questioning is relevant," said the judge.

"What I can say is that I have reasonable grounds to believe that it will lead to relevant evidence," said Dure.

"If you were a younger lawyer," said the judge, "I meant to say, a less experienced lawyer, I would be tempted to sustain the objection, if only to protect your client. But you are an experienced defense attorney and I will give you substantial latitude. I hope you don't hang yourself with it – or your client. Objection overruled."

The lawyers and the court reporter returned to their places, and the judge scooted his wheeled judge's chair back to his place behind the middle of the bench.

"How about groundhogs?" said Dure. "Have you seen groundhogs run over in the road around your house?"

This question seemed to startle the witness. Warily he said, "Yes."

"Now, on account of all this roadkill, isn't it a fact that buzzards are also common in your neighborhood?"

"You mean vultures," said Loveless.

"I said 'buzzards.' Isn't it a fact that buzzards are common in your neighborhood?"

"Vultures are common," said Loveless. "'Buzzards' is a vague term used by the ignorant." He tried to suppress a smirk of superiority.

"You are informed about birds, I take it?" said Dure.

Loveless gave a shrug of modesty. "I know something about them."

"In fact, you have been what is commonly know as a 'bird-watcher'?"

A slightly less emphatic shrug. "Yes," said Loveless.

"In fact, you used to roam about your neighborhood with field glasses, isn't that right?"

A note of hostility crept into Loveless's voice. He sat up straighter and compressed his lips. "Yes," he said.

"But you stopped doing that when a woman accused you of being a peeping Tom?" said Dure.

"Objection!" said Preston.

"Approach the bench, gentlemen," said the judge, wearily.

"Your Honor," said Preston, when they had all assembled, "not only have we not seen any relevant testimony, now Mr. Dure is attempting to expose this witness to ridicule. It is unethical and the questions are irrelevant. I object."

"And I object to Mr. Preston's uncivil and improper tactic of continually interrupting the flow of cross-examination. As Your Honor knows, the exposure of biased or dishonest testimony is an art, and it depends on the flow of questions and the atmosphere created by the cross-examiner. That is why the law frowns on repeated interruptions of cross-examination. This line of questioning is proceeding exactly as I anticipated it would, and we will soon get some traction, if Mr. Preston will stop his improper objections."

The judge sighed. "Since this is a murder case, I am going to allow the defense latitude – reluctantly. You will keep in mind, Mr. Dure, that you can alienate the jury as well as the Court if all of this leads to nothing."

Nobody said anything further, and the little conclave broke up.

"Let me rephrase the question," said Dure. "Didn't some misguided woman object to your walking around the neighborhood with field glasses in your hands?"

"Something of that nature, yes."

"In fact, you never had interest in what might have been going on in any of the houses, you were only observing birds, isn't that right?"

"Yes, that's right."

"And after that encounter with that woman, you left off using the neighborhood as a birding ground?"

"That is true."

"How many years have you been watching birds?"

"Perhaps twenty?" offered Loveless.

Dure put his next question with a friendly manner, as if giving the witness a chance to brag. "How many birds on your life list?"

Loveless seemed surprised by the question and a little suspicious. "I have to agree with Mr. Preston that I don't see what this has to do with anything, but I think it is about 347."

"The witness will answer the question," said the judge sternly, "and leave the objections to the lawyers."

"Are you the kind of birder," said Dure, "who can spot a tiny tit sixty feet up in the branches of a tree?"

"Well actually, you would rarely see a tit that high up. They are more commonly found from ten to twenty-five feet up. But, yes, I am pretty good at spotting birds."

"Tell us then," said Dure, "why is it that you did not notice the vultures with a six-foot wing span landing and feeding and leaving just thirty feet from your bedroom window all during the weekend of June 5 through 7?"

A brief frisson of shock could be observed in Loveless. He cleared his throat. "What was the question?" he said.

Dure repeated it.

"I didn't notice any vultures probably because there weren't any," said Loveless.

"Suppose I told you that Dr. McCann, the Commonwealth's medical examiner, had testified that vultures had been feeding on the corpse for at least twenty-four hours before it was discovered?"

"So?" said Loveless. "I didn't see any."

"So you're a birding enthusiast who can spot a tiny tit in a tall tree, but you weren't able to notice huge vultures landing thirty feet from your bedroom window?"

During the course of Dure's cross-examination, the atmosphere in the courtroom had been growing tenser. The usual rustling, whispering, coughing, and creaking of benches and chairs in the courtroom had ceased. Even Preston was rapt, literally sitting on the edge of his seat. It was so quiet that one might have heard a spider spinning its web.

"Nope, didn't see it," said Loveless.

"All weekend you did not see any vulture landing or taking off next door?"

"Nope."

"Do you keep the shades drawn in your bedroom during the day?" asked Dure.

"I might have that weekend."

"But it's not a habit with you?"

Loveless swayed slightly in his chair before answering. "No," he finally said.

"When I inspected the scene on that late Monday afternoon, June 8, my assistant took photographs, one of which shows that window with no shades drawn."

"Okay," said Loveless.

"You are suggesting that normally you do not draw the shades during the day, but you might have done so on that particular weekend?"

"I might have had my sleep schedule discombobulated," said Loveless.

"Perhaps by some illicit nighttime activity?" suggested Dure.

Loveless seemed annoyed. "I don't know what you are trying to suggest," he said.

"You testified that you had overheard quarrels between Mrs. Houlihan and Mr. Houlihan?"

"Yes."

"I think you testified that the most recent argument you overheard was 'loud' and 'violent'?"

"Yes."

"And you could hear her voice from her yard to yours?"

"Yes."

"So her voice was loud?"

"Yes."

"And violent?" said Dure.

"I don't know what you mean by 'violent'." said Loveless.

"It's your word. You testified that the argument was 'loud' and 'violent.'"

"They were arguing violently."

"Were you watching them, or only hearing them?"

"I could not see, but only hear."

"And when you testified on direct, you only mentioned her voice, isn't that right?"

"I don't recall."

"Should we read back the transcript?"

"Her voice stood out. He either said nothing, or spoke so low that I just heard a mumble."

"So it would be fair to say, that based on your perception, Mrs. Houlihan could at times use her voice in a manner that was loud and violent."

"Okay."

"In fact, you had personal experience of Mrs. Houlihan's loud and violent voice, didn't you?"

Loveless made a slight gesture with his shoulders, twice in quick succession. He seemed uncertain how to answer. Then he smiled and said, "She did get upset on one occasion."

Now it was Dure's turn to hesitate. He stared at the legal pad he was holding in his hand and made a moue. Then he said, "What occasion was that?" But before Loveless could answer, he said, "Strike the question. In fact, it was on an occasion when you were burning some branches in your backyard?"

"Yes," said Loveless.

"Within the past two years?"

"Yes."

"She came into your yard screaming?"

"I would say she was upset."

"And in fact, she threatened to report you to the police, didn't she?"

Loveless pressed his lips together before answering. "She may have. I don't recall everything that was said."

"And didn't you threaten to have her arrested for trespassing?"

"Again, I don't recall everything that was said."

"You don't deny it?"

"I don't recall exactly."

"So you cannot deny that you threatened to have her arrested for trespassing in your yard?"

"I don't know what your source of information is."

"That is now the third time you have failed to deny that you threatened to have her arrested for trespassing in your yard. We understand."

Dure stood still for a long moment, and silent. He stepped to the clerk's table and took up the baggie with the bullet in it.

"May I approach the witness?" said Dure to the judge.

"Go ahead."

Dure showed the baggie with its enclosed bullet to Loveless. "Have you seen this before?"

Loveless barely glanced at it. "No," he said dismissively.

Dure walked slowly back to the clerk's table and put the baggie down. He turned.

"Mr. Loveless, you are aware that the prosecution has not disavowed the death penalty in this case?"

"I don't know. It's not something that concerns me."

"So that if the defendant, Mr. Houlihan, should be convicted, he might be put to death?"

Loveless snorted a kind of 'hmmpf.' "He was the one who confessed, not me."

Instead of asking another question, Dure stared at Loveless for a long moment. Then he said, "No, you haven't confessed, have you? So we have one potential outcome of this trial is that Liam Houlihan would become an orphan?"

Loveless shrugged his shoulders and looked away.

Dure did not insist on an answer, but went on to his next question. All during this series of questions, Preston had been half springing up from his chair and then subsiding, as if he wanted to object, but each time at the last second decided not to.

Dure asked, "Not only an orphan, but an orphaned young man who would be convinced that his father murdered his mother?"

"Don't bother me about it. Mr. Houlihan confessed and there's an end of the matter."

"Obviously not the end of the matter, since we are here, talking about what happened. You're seventy years old, right?"

"Yes."

"Objection, Your Honor." Preston finally was standing.

Yet another conclave took place at the judge's bench. Several jurors rolled their eyes.

"Your Honor!" said Preston, in a tone of aggrievement, "this cross-examination is beyond all bounds. The questions are irrelevant, incompetent, argumentative, beyond the scope of direct examination, and simply unprofessional."

Dure stood silent and patient to the extent that the judge had to ask him for his answer to the objection. Dure's hazel eyes were beginning to blaze and he spoke with restrained heat. "What I have to say, Your Honor already knows. Cross-examination is an engine to ferret out the truth. Sometimes, as in this case, it is the only thing that an innocent defendant has to protect himself from wrongful conviction. It is in criminal trials a sacred right." (Preston pressed his lips tightly together, and looked away in disgust.) "The prosecution is determined to deny the defendant this right by running interference for the witness, disrupting the examination with repeated objections. None of my questions is objectionable. The total import of the series of questions is intended to be non-obvious to the witness. Perhaps my learned friend also does not see where this is leading – or, if he does, then his repeated objections are truly despicable."

The judge said, "I am not pleased with the performance of either of you. I guess we will see how things turn out when the jury returns with a verdict. At the moment, it seems to me that Mr. Dure is doing as much harm to his client's case as good, and I am going to let things play out. I think that both of your complaints have merit: Mr. Dure, your questions do seem far-fetched and borderline abusive – but again, I am going to give you leeway because this is cross-examination in a capital case. Mr. Preston, I will allow you to have a standing objection based on relevance, on this condition: that at the next break, you bring to the court's attention that question or those questions with respect to which you wish to press your objection, and we will settle those matters when next the jury is taken out."

Again the players returned to their places.

"You are seventy years old?" asked Dure.

"Yes," said Loveless.

"Did you know that the appeals process in death-penalty cases often take ten years or more?"

"No."

"How old was your father when he died?"

"What does that matter?" said Loveless, with resentment.

"Answer the question," said Dure.

At the prosecution table, Preston was shaking his head.

Loveless turned to look up at the judge, who in answer to Loveless's mute appeal, said, "Answer the question."

"Sixty-six."

"And your mother?"

"Sixty-five."

"Did you ever think you were on borrowed time?"

"No," said Loveless, but it was apparent that he gave no thought to the answer, but was simply refusing to go along with anything Dure might suggest.

"Liam Houlihan is twenty-three years old," said Dure. "How long is it from age twenty-three to age seventy?"

Loveless became briefly pensive. "Not that long," he said in a soft voice.

"How long would it be if someone thought that his father had murdered his mother?"

Loveless shrugged his shoulders. "I wouldn't know," he said.

"Mr. Loveless, you do own a firearm, don't you?"

Loveless's body twitched and he looked at Dure. Without moving his head, let his eyes slide over to look at Houlihan. Houlihan, at the defense table, was staring back at Loveless. Loveless swayed slightly in the chair. He inhaled sharply and stared now at the front railing of the witness box. Finally, he settled back in the witness chair and said nothing.

"You own a .22 rifle. Isn't that right?" said Dure.

Loveless pressed his lips together, inhaled again sharply, and settled his shoulders back in the chair, saying nothing.

"You do own a .22 rifle. It has a scope mounted on it?" said Dure.

Loveless turned to look at Houlihan and a faint smile of comprehension came on his lips. He seemed to make up his mind. "I did at one time," he said.

"The report from a .22 is not very loud, is it?"

"It's loud enough to wear ear protection," said Loveless.

"You wear hearing protection when you fire it indoors, I take it?" said Dure.

Loveless gave a start and blinked. "Anyone would," he said.

"Where you live, with the large lots and the trees, it's not likely that the report of a .22, even if fired outdoors would be noticed, is it?"

"I think it would."

"But if it were fired indoors, say through an open window, and at a time when loud lawnmowers were operating in the neighborhood, it's not likely that anyone would notice it?"

"I don't know how one would know that," said Loveless.

"In this case, it appears that no one did, isn't that right?"

Loveless was beginning to slump slightly, to subside in the chair in which he was sitting. "Did what?" he said.

"No one noticed the firing of a .22 from your bedroom through your open bedroom window while loud lawnmowers were operating in the Sweets' yard across the street?"

Loveless let out a deep sigh. "No."

Dure picked up the baggie with the bullet in it. He did not ask the judge's permission, but went to the witness box and held it out to Loveless. "This bullet came from your rifle, didn't it."

"No," said Loveless, weakly, but his head was nodding as if to say 'yes.'

"You shot Mrs. Houlihan, and now, you are tired, and you are old, and you do not want to make a second murder by allowing an innocent man to be convicted. And maybe it was a mistake, or a crime of opportunity, I don't know, but whatever justification you had, you did not foresee this, you did not sign up for this, you do not want to commit the cowardly and despicable deception of making a young man think his father killed his mother. You'll have a chance to explain yourself, maybe even to justify yourself, but right now you have to say that you did it." Dure stood silent, expectantly, as the whole courtroom was silent, and the air of expectation was heavy.

Loveless was breathing heavily. His head sagged and softly he voiced the words, "Alright . . . yes."

It took a moment for the import of this utterance to be realized by the courtroom. Murmuring began throughout the courtroom. The judge rapped the bench with his gavel. Preston sat with a peculiar expression on his face, as if he had opened a gift-wrapped box and found something revolting inside. He rose and went with Dure to a sidebar conference.

"Your Honor," said Preston "the Commonwealth would like to *nol pros* this case at this time."

"The defense will not object," said Dure, "so long as the dismissal is with prejudice."

"Your Honor, the Commonwealth cannot agree to that," said Preston. "Supposing this testimony should be recanted, the Commonwealth must retain the right to re-institute charges against this defendant."

"In that case, Your Honor," said Dure, "the defense insists that this trial go to verdict."

Preston looked at Dure with annoyance. Disgust showed on his aristocratic features. "In the absence of any cooperation from defense counsel," he said, "the Commonwealth requests that the trial be adjourned for a week, so that further investigation can be done."

"We object to that," said Dure. "It would be a great inconvenience for the witnesses and the jury, and a violation of the defendant's speedy trial right."

The judge asked, "How many days has it been? Is there any danger of a speedy trial violation?"

"None whatever," said Preston. "We are well within the guidelines."

"The defense maintains," said Dure, "that a delay during trial of that magnitude is a separate violation of speedy trial rights, independent of the total time of the prosecution, as well as a violation of due process because of the effect on the jury of loss of recollection of evidence, and risk of contamination by extra-judicial information."

The judge said, "As you know, once the jury has been sworn, the Court cannot dismiss the case over the defendant's objection. What I'm going to do is this: The court will adjourn until 10:00 tomorrow morning. At that time, the case will proceed to verdict, unless the prosecution agrees to a dismissal with prejudice."

14.

The next morning, at 9:05, Dure received a telephone call from Preston. Preston said that the police had intensively interrogated Loveless, that he had signed a confession, and that the case against Houlihan would be dismissed with prejudice. Over the next fifteen minutes the two lawyers agreed by e-mail on the wording of a stipulation and order of dismissal. At ten o'clock, the order was presented to the judge, who signed it and discharged the jury with his thanks.

The winning of a murder case is such a powerful thrill that it even overcame Dure's constitutional glumness for a day. He had an extra bounce in his step which made his gait awkward and slightly ridiculous, as if he were hurrying through a tall-grass meadow to meet someone special; and even though from his lack of sleep the bags under his eyes were larger and grayer than ever, his eyes themselves glowed golden.

The Monday after the trial, Houlihan stopped in to say thank you in a fuller manner than the fumbling utterances he could manage at the trial. He was dressed in neat civilian clothes. Kara showed him into Dure's office.

"*Now* I know why people say you're the best lawyer in town," he said as he entered. His voice was clearer and stronger.

Dure took the praise with a grimace; he did not smile. He invited Houlihan to sit.

"I was shocked that it was Everett Loveless," said Houlihan. "But then I thought: we had become somewhat estranged over the past few years. We had been friendly neighbors at one time."

Dure nodded, said nothing.

"How did you know that it was him?" asked Houlihan.

"It was a complex process which culminated in cross-examination with a prepared mind," said Dure. "It was observation, elimination, and pondering." Dure sat back in his chair. "First of all, I believed that you did not do it. That meant someone else did it. You look for motive, opportunity, lack of alibi. This was a tough case because the time of death could not be pinpointed. That meant opportunity and lack of alibi were not useful clues. That meant the focus had to be on motive, but there didn't seem to be any strong motive. Even as trial began, I had suspicions as to who did it, but I did not know. The key turned out to be post-crime efforts to evade detection. If Loveless had not planted the head in your trailer, which led to the discovery of the bullet, he might have gotten away with the crime." A strange look came over Dure's face. "I should charge you double the fee," he said, "because your ignoring my advice made the case three time harder than it would have been."

"Huh?" said Houlihan with an expression of panic on his face.

"I told you not to talk about the case with anyone, then you go and talk about the case – with the police no less." Dure seemed disgusted.

"I'm sorry about that," said Houlihan.

Dure was silent, seeming to stew in irritation. Houlihan was sweating. Finally Dure said, "Okay. I'll let it go. All's swell that ends swell."

Houlihan smiled involuntarily and relaxed. "But how did you know that it was Loveless?" he asked.

"Not until I was cross-examining him was I sure. In that very intense interaction you have to read the person you are cross-examining. With knowledge of the facts you probe – but it's a matter of judgment which witness to probe and how much – it can blow up in your face. You probe and you read the witness and adjust your attack as you progress. Remember the Audubon on Loveless's coffee table? And the story of his bird watching in the neighborhood? That didn't add up with his not having noticed vultures in the next yard. So I was suspicious of him. When the prosecution brought in the head and the bullet, then it was clear how the murder was done. And then it was just a matter of probing and provoking the witness, and reading the signs. When I asked him if he owned a firearm and he twitched, that told me I was on the right track."

The telephone rang. Kara answered it. "It's for you," she said to Dure. "Roderick Preston."

Dure looked meaningfully at Houlihan and took up the receiver.

"Walter? This is Roderick Preston."

"Yes, Roderick, I recognize your voice."

"Ahem, regarding the Houlihan case, Cliff Whittaker is defending Mr. Loveless."

"You have my sympathy."

"Well, thanks. I was wondering if, in the interest of justice, you might help me out a bit?"

"Hang on a minute. I'm sitting here with Mr. Houlihan. Let me put you on the speaker."

"I guess it's alright," said Preston, sounding unenthused.

Dure said, "Okay. Whatever I can do to further the cause of justice . . . ."

"I appreciate that," said Preston. "In plea negotiations with Mr. Whittaker, he's arguing that because your client Houlihan confessed to the murder, the Commonwealth will never be able to prove guilt beyond a reasonable doubt as to Loveless, because the defense will produce your client's confession to the same crime, and that will be enough to give rise to reasonable doubt."

"Hmm, not a bad argument."

"So, I'm going to need your client to testify as to how he made a false confession."

"How do you know that my client did make a false confession?" asked Dure, with a mischievous gleam in his eye.

"Before Mr. Loveless retained Whittaker to represent him, he was cooperative," said Preston, sounding put out. "He explained what he did in convincing detail which is corroborated by the physical evidence which we retrieved from his house and garage."

"We're dying to hear the details," said Dure.

"I'll tell you if you'll tell me something."

"What's that?" said Dure.

"How you opened Mrs. Houlihan's phone."

"Okay, that's a deal if you go first," said Dure.

"Loveless was greatly annoyed by the groundhogs that Mr. Houlihan tolerated on his property. They used to come over to Loveless's house and eat his garden plants and start digging holes. So, Loveless would shoot them with his .22 rifle. But to keep anyone in the neighborhood from finding out, he would only do his shooting when the landscape crews were mowing in the neighborhood. As you suggested, the sound of the mowers camouflaged the sound of the shots. So, when the mowers came, Loveless would set up his rifle in his bedroom and shoot out the window if he happened to see a groundhog in his yard or on the boundary line between the yards. On the day in question, he was watching for a groundhog when Mrs. Houlihan came into view. Apparently old resentments came to the surface and he took advantage of the opportunity. He hadn't planned to do it – at least so he claims. After he fired the shot, he was afraid that the police would be able to use the bullet in the head to tie him to the murder, so he used a hacksaw to cut off the head and took it to his garage. He wanted to extract the bullet before disposing of the head, but he decided it would be too messy and difficult to extract the bullet. He thought about it a couple of days and finally used a blowtorch to heat up the shaft of a screwdriver from which he had cut the handle off. He put the shaft in the bullet hole and kept it long enough to deform or melt the bullet so that it could not be matched to his gun.

"It's ironic that all of this effort did not really matter in the end because it was not by ballistics that he was found out. But he could not decide how to get rid of the head. When Houlihan confessed, he felt the pressure was off. Then, when you made such a big deal at trial of the police not having found the head, he snuck over to Houlihan's house and planted the head in Houlihan's shave-ice trailer. He thought he was killing two birds with one stone: getting rid of the head, and making sure that Houlihan would be convicted.

"We recovered a .22 rifle from his house and found evidence in his garage to corroborate this, including a screwdriver handle with no shaft, and burnt remains in a portable grill of plastic gloves, a plastic bag and other paraphernalia he had used to do his dirty work.

"So the conclusion is, we are convinced that he did it and that your client – God knows why – gave a false confession. So, now, you'll help the Commonwealth defeat Mr. Whittaker's gambit? . . . Oh, but first, how did you open that phone?"

Here Dure burst out laughing in a way that was uncharacteristic and seemed inappropriate. It was a horse laugh out of which the arc of his upper teeth was fully visible. Belatedly, he put his hand over his mouth. After a moment the laugh subsided. "Mr. Houlihan will remember, but you of course could not know. He signed an authorization to have the body exhumed, which I did to test for poisons in the body – at that time, no one knew, or at least we did not know, how the murder had been committed. While the body was up, I had the right thumb carefully tumefied with a saline solution. Then an impression was taken and a thin silicon membrane created of her thumbprint. I wore this on my thumb . . . and it worked to activate the phone's touch ID. So, no big mystery."

There was a moment of silence from the other end of the line. "I see," said Preston finally.

Houlihan spoke up. He seemed to be feeling confident and expansive. "What was the hissing voicemail message on Mr. Parker's phone?"

Preston answered this. The alacrity in his voice showed that he was glad of this opportunity to try to catch up with Dure in the perduring competition among lawyers to demonstrate knowledge and competence. "We determined that the default setting on Mrs. Houlihan's phone, which she hadn't changed, was that missed calls could be returned even while the phone was locked. As you know, we took possession of

Parker's phone and found out that he had called her at 6:56 p.m. Loveless waited until dark, around 9:30, to go out in the yard with his hacksaw. My hypothesis is that in disturbing the corpse, he caused a pocket dial that returned Parker's call."

"A brilliant deduction, Roderick," said Dure.

"And now," said Preston, "I imagine that Mr. Houlihan would like to see the real murderer of his wife convicted of his crime. So I can't imagine that there would be any resistance to his testifying for the prosecution."

"I expect you're right, Roderick," said Dure. "But I'll discuss it with my client."

"Keep in mind," said Preston, "that making a false report to the police is a crime, even a false confession. But I will be willing to overlook the matter if Mr. Houlihan cooperates in the prosecution of Loveless."

"In this case, Roderick, there's a clear defense of entrapment. That would take the cake: the police use questionable methods to coerce a confession, and then prosecute the innocent party for making a false report to the police! But I'll discuss the matter of testifying with my client. I think I can persuade him."

"That would be good," said Preston.

There was a pause in the conversation. Then Dure asked, "Roderick, what are you charging Loveless with?"

"Murder in the first degree."

"Is that it?"

"What else could there be?"

"If you want some leverage in negotiating with our friend Mr. Whittaker, you might suggest that you are considering adding another count: you might charge Loveless with attempted murder."

"Attempted murder? I don't get it."

"By lying and committing perjury, he tried to put my client to death. Seems like an attempt to murder to me. Murder by judicial process."

"I'll consider that."

"You *were* asking for the death penalty."

"That's true."

"Maybe you can persuade Mr. Whittaker to a reasonable plea bargain – then you won't have to impeach your police as to how they wangled a false confession out of my client."

"Whenever I talk with you, Walter, I learn something."

"Iron sharpens iron. Good bye." Dure hung up the phone and gave Houlihan one of his rare smiles.

THE END.

Do you have a reaction to share?

If you enjoyed reading this book, the publisher and author would appreciate your posting a review on your favorite on-line bookseller to help other readers.

Your support is appreciated.

Don't Miss The Next "Hard Case"

Successful, middle-aged businessman Richard Hargrave owns a health club. He hires stunning, statuesque, 23-year old Vanessa as a trainer. In due course he divorces his wife, Elizabeth, to marry Vanessa. Elizabeth asks for the health club in the divorce settlement and Richard agrees, on the condition that Elizabeth keep Vanessa on as a trainer. Richard, knowing that both women will continue to love him, keeps his membership as well, and when he visits the health club, relations among the three seem to be cordial. Out of this situation arises *The Case of the Unhealthy Health Club*, another hard case for attorney Walter Dure.

Made in the USA
Middletown, DE
13 November 2021